HIGHLAND
SEDUCTION

ANNA JONES

THE *Erotic* Print Society
London 2004
Printed and bound in Spain by Bookprint
S.L., Barcelona

THE *Erotic* Print Society
EPS, 1 Maddox Street
LONDON W1S 2PZ

Tel (UK only): 0871 7110 134
Fax: +44 (0)20 7437 3528
Email: eros@eroticprints.org
Web: www.eroticprints.org

© 2004 MacHo Ltd, London UK

ISBN : 1-898998-83-3

HIGHLAND SEDUCTION

ANNA JONES

THE *Erotic* Print Society

Foreword by Michael R. Goss

The history of erotic literature had always been clandestine, and, apart from furtive purchases of under-the-counter hardcore, American readers between the end of the war and the mid-1960s could only openly buy paperbacks with lurid covers that always promised, like first dates, far more than they actually delivered. However, the sale of two trashy paperbacks at a newsstand in New York's Times Square was to change the history of erotic publishing in the United States forever.

Previously there had been several landmark cases involving the publication of books that extended the boundaries of what was legally acceptable. These included James Joyce's *Ulysses*, D.H. Lawrence's *Lady Chatterley's Lover*, Henry Miller's *Tropic of Cancer*, John Cleland's *Memoirs of a Woman of Pleasure* and William Burrough's *Naked Lunch*. All novels which today we celebrate and study as major works of literature.

The pivotal moment came when Robert Redrup, a Times Square newsstand clerk, sold two pulp sex novels, *Lust Pool* and *Shame Agent* to plain-clothes policeman, for which he was tried and convicted in 1965. William Hamling, who published the books under his Nightstand imprint in San Diego, paid Redrup's legal bills to the Supreme Court and the resulting case, *Redrup v. New York* in May 1967, truly opened the floodgates of what was acceptable.

Hamling, and his lawyer Stanley Fleishman, firmly believed that he was not selling, as was said about his books, "commercialised obscenity," nor would he admit to "titillating the prurient interests of people with a weakness for such expression." Hamling felt his books were giving people who would never have the skills to read and enjoy *Ulysses*, *Fanny Hill* or *Naked Lunch* what they wanted.

The judge presiding over the case of Redrup, Justice Potter Stewart, went far beyond his established just-left-of-centre position on obscenity to the most radical of outlooks. Apparently the vote to affirm Ralph Ginzburg's conviction for his magazine *Eros* was his personal wake-up call. In his Ginzburg summary Stewart wrote:

Censorship reflects a society's lack of confidence in itself. It is a hallmark of an authoritarian regime. Long ago those who wrote our First Amendment charted a different course. They believed a society can be truly strong only when it is truly free. In the realm of expression they put their faith, for better or worse, in the enlightened choice of the people, free from the interference of a policeman's intrusive thumb or a judge's heavy hand. So it is that the Constitution protects coarse expression as well as refined, and vulgarity no less than elegance. A book worthless to me may convey something of value to my neighbour. In the free society to which our Constitution has committed us, it is for each to choose for himself.

Stewart's arguments were persuasive enough to convince the court to reverse Redrup's original conviction by 7-2. This decision by the United States Supreme Court affirmed that consenting adults ought to be constitutionally entitled, under the First Amendment, to acquire and read any publication that they wished, including those agreed to be obscene or pornographic, free of interference from the U.S. Government.

Under this guiding principle the Supreme Court adopted a policy of systematically reversing without further opinion ("Redruping") all obscenity convictions which reached it. Scores of obscenity rulings involving paperback sex books, girlie magazines and peep shows were overturned.

Despite an attempt to reverse the tide of pornography by new Chief Justice

Warren E. Burger in the 1970s an explosion in paperback publishing followed. Carpetbagger publishers burst into life across America, including Brandon House, Essex House, Greenleaf, Lancer, Midwood, Pendulum, Pleasure Readers, Star Distributors and many others. Every aspect of human sexuality was covered in a sexual anarchy of threesomes, foursomes and more-somes in every combination of genders and colours, often including the whole family, their pets and assorted farm animals to boot. Every genre was exploited from incest to Nazi sex with everything in-between in a total assault on the values of bourgeois culture. One can imagine publishers and authors sitting in bars coming up with titles in alcohol-and-dope-fuelled brainstorming sessions which would then be commissioned out to a stable of jobbing hacks for around $500 a book.

Past Venus Press will reissue the highlights from this post-Redrup period, many of which were originally considered to have had no literary merit whatsoever and to be utterly without redeeming social importance. But that, of course, was part of their charm.

Chapter 1

A thick fog enveloped the airport terminal, blocking out the hopeful early morning light. It was eight-thirty in the morning, and in the departure lounge, waiting for the boarding announcement, a young woman and her husband tenderly kissed their goodbyes. The young woman, tall, blonde and strikingly attractive, watched the grey wisps of fog with apprehensive eyes and clung tightly to the man's lean, muscular arm. "Will your plane be able to take off in all that fog, darling?" she hopefully whispered to him. "I don't see how it can; you can hardly see anything at all."

Alex Langley, confidently dressed in a well-cut brown suit, grinned and gently pinched his wife's cheek. "Silly baby," he said sweetly, "you don't have to worry about a thing. Flying in weather like this is very normal. They wouldn't let us take off if it wasn't safe."

"I know," Amanda said quietly, "but you know how nervous I am about flying anyway. And this weather..."

"You worry too much," Alex chided gently.

"Well, maybe I do, but I love you and I don't want anything to happen to you."

"Nothing's going to happen to me, baby doll," he said. "This is just a simple, routine business trip to Genoa. I'll be back with you in a few days, and you'll have all my attention."

"I know, but..."

"No buts, now. I want none of this fretting; I want you to be enjoying yourself with Isabelle, letting your hair down. I'm sure you're going to have a lot of fun, and remember, she's the boss's wife."

"Oh, you don't have to worry about me making a good impression," Amanda said with a hint of petulance. "I won't do anything to put you in a bad light."

"Honey, you know I didn't mean anything like that."

Amanda felt embarrassed suddenly of her worries and fears over a simple plane flight and a few days away on a business trip. She put her arms around her husband and clung to him tightly, kissing him openly, unmindful of the crowd of people waiting to board the aircraft or saying goodbye to friends and relatives.

Oh, how she loved him, she thought as she nuzzled his broad chest. They had been married almost three years now, but her ardour for the man she had chosen from a long, long list of suitors back in America had not waned in the slightest since their wedding day. She looked up at him to study his manly, rugged features, his eyes betraying the tenderness he had inside. Three or four days seemed to her to be such a long time. From the moment they had been married in the small, stone church in Cuyama in Santa Barbara, they had been separated for only a few hours at a time, certainly never more than a single day. They had lived the small-town life for a while, pleasuring in their home and their private times together. Then Alex got the job offer from England, a great opportunity to work for Mediterranean Containers Ltd, one of the biggest shipping companies in Europe, and they flew to England together to sign the two-year contract.

They had lived in London now for the better part of a year, in a small flat in Paddington, and she had been deliriously happy. The English people fascinated her, and she felt at ease around them; she and Alex had made many friends during their stay, and had become very popular in their middle-class social circle. They were an active couple, doing many things together – tennis, swimming, hiking, horse riding – and they were completely compatible in every way.

Their lovemaking, from the very first (Amanda had been a virgin on their wedding night, and Alex had had only a few brief interludes with women of questionable standing), had been tender and gentle, and yet somehow abandoned too. They never ceased to satisfy each other, Amanda thought, and she blushed slightly as she remembered the feel of Alex's large, rigid penis filling her vagina the night before, and the passion with which she had urged him on to greater thrusts deep inside her to bring about the glorious splendour of their eventual and simultaneous orgasms.

Amanda sighed, kissing her husband again and snuggling up into the embrace of his strong arms. No, she needed nothing else from life except this man – and he needed nothing else except her. These next few days, even though they had been promised to be both adventuresome and relaxing by Isabelle Palermo, would be empty for Amanda until Alex returned.

She had become good friends with Isabelle, the wife of Sebastian Palermo, the Vice-President in charge of Sales at Mediterranean Containers Ltd and Alex's immediate superior, during the past year. Isabelle, young, vivacious and beautiful, 20 years her husband's junior, had that kind of magnetism that instantly drew people to her. Amanda, who was much quieter and much more conservative, didn't really approve of some of Isabelle's habits or traits, but she liked the Englishwoman nonetheless.

Two days ago, when Alex had told her he was flying to Genoa with Sebastian Palermo on business, the beautiful young wife had experienced a feeling of loss at the thought of their separation. But then Alex had said that she would not have to be alone during his absence in Italy, and that she and Isabelle could spend the time together at the estate of James Figgis – Sandaig Manor – in Knoydart in a remote part of the Scottish Highlands. Figgis, a wealthy young man of aristocratic background and long-time friend of the Palermos, had invited the two wives – and Alex and Sebastian when they returned from Genoa – to be his guests for as long as they cared to stay.

Amanda had met James Figgis on two separate occasions at small cocktail gatherings in the Palermo home, and had found him a charming, intelligent and attractive man; the invitation had been appealing to her, and later, when she had spoken to Isabelle and learned the facts surrounding Sandaig Manor, she had readily accepted the gracious proposal.

The ancestral home of the young heir to a vast fortune was isolated, the nearest neighbour being over four miles away, and while offering that hint of forbidden mystery intimated by its location, it also offered luxury and relaxation in its stately and baronial rooms and halls. Both attributes appealed to the young wife's nature, and she was looking forward to the journey to Knoydart with Isabelle in the Palermos' new Mercedes – but she wished that her husband were going to be with them at Sandaig Manor for their entire stay there, and not just the last couple of days of it.

Alex Langley held his soft, sweet young wife for a moment longer, then stood her away from him gently and looked into her lovely face. He never tired of looking at her, at the fine, symmetrically formed features, the small, pert nose and the wide, guileless blue eyes, the soft, round mouth and the long, cascading silkiness of her honey-blonde hair falling about the shoulders of her plaid raincoat. Her full, firm, voluptuous breasts jutted forth with feminine allure from under her coat, and he glimpsed their smooth curves between the open buttons. He surreptitiously slid his hand inside her coat to feel those beautiful breasts and she gasped slightly, her nipples responding to his touch. He withdrew and moved his hand down onto her firm, round buttocks, which were provocatively outlined by her fitted coat. She was a woman in a thousand, a million, he thought possessively; he was an incredibly lucky man to have a wife like Amanda, very damn lucky.

He touched her lightly under the chin. "You'll have a wonderful time in Knoydart, sweetheart," he told her. "But I don't want you going off by yourself on those hills. It can be dangerous out there without someone along who knows his way around."

"I'll be careful," she promised.

"That's my girl."

"It really is going to be fun," said Amanda, her eyes lighting with renewed excitement, her mind momentarily off the impending flight and separation. "Just think, Alex: a real old Scottish estate in the wild Scottish highlands! I feel like... well, like Jane Eyre or somebody."

Alex laughed. "I'm kind of looking forward to it myself, all right. But if you hear any howling beasts in the middle of the night, don't you dare go out to investigate!"

She poked his arm lightly. "Oh, you!"

He sobered for a moment, kissing her again and peering into her eyes. "You will have a good time, won't you? I'll be thinking about you all the while I'm in Italy."

"And I about you, darling," she replied. "But I'll have a good time, I know I will."

In the corner of the lounge, Isabelle and Sebastian stood talking in low tones about the days ahead of them. Both revelled in the simple sexuality of the couple they wished to devour and, had Amanda and Alex heard what was in store for them at Sandaig Manor, they would have been horrified. Never in their wildest imaginations would they have imagined the dark and licentious acts these two outwardly normal, respectable people were plotting.

Isabelle Palermo – smallish, pert, just past thirty – stood very close to her greying, distinguished, somewhat portly mate, her dark eyes flashing with a usually hidden intensity. Her black, close-cropped hair shone with reddish highlights in the strong light of the airport waiting area, and her generous red mouth was quirked into a smile of anticipation and delight. As she spoke, she ran her hands seductively over his chest, and occasionally moved down slightly to let her fingers stray caressingly over his penis through his suit.

"Yes, everything is arranged with James," Isabelle was saying softly. "He's given all his servants the week off, all except Ganfeld, of course. And he has all the necessary items we'll need for a complete subjugation of dear, sweet Amanda."

"Good, good," enthused Sebastian, his brown eyes showing their approval of his wife; he never stopped marvelling at the depths of her wantonness, so carefully hidden from public view – wantonness, and yes, her streak of sadistic delight in the debauching of young, innocent women like Alex Langley's wife. "I'll keep Alex in Genoa about three days. That ought to give you enough time, especially if Genghis is up to his old tricks," he chuckled lewdly, almost inaudibly.

"James – and Ganfeld – will see to that," Isabelle told him.

"Ganfeld," Sebastian chuckled almost sardonically. "Sometimes I shudder when I think of that ugly little man's penis inside your fine belly, my sweet. Promise me you won't suck him while you're at the Manor."

"I won't make any such promise at all," Isabelle said, her eyes gleaming. "You know how much I like the taste of a man in my mouth, and the feel of his massive cock in my pussy."

Sebastian sighed. "I suppose I'll have to console myself with the thought of getting my own cock – and my tongue, too! – between the soft, silky thighs of Mrs Amanda Langley."

As Sebastian spoke, he slipped his hand down Isabelle's skirt and into her panties. "I am going to be so jealous of you all and what you'll get up to while I'm away," he said, inserting a finger into her pussy and bringing it out, wet, to excite her clit.

Isabelle leaned against him and felt herself quivering as he moved the finger back and forth on her clit. "Sebastian, you naughty thing!" she whispered. "You are going to have to expend a bit of that energy while you're in Italy. Not too much, though; we need you ripe and ready for her when you return."

"She's not going to be an easy one to conquer," Sebastian mused. "She's devoted to Alex, and she's intelligent too."

"Just leave things to James and Ganfeld and me, oh, and of course, Genghis, my pet," said Isabelle. "I've cultivated that young beauty long enough; the time is ripe for action."

"You know best, Isabelle," Sebastian said, gathering her into his arms, pressing her firm, rounded body tight against his and continuing to rub her erect and wet clitoris as he spoke. "You never fail me – or yourself – do you?"

"Never," she replied, nipping and sucking at his ear. "Mrs Amanda Langley will be a new woman indeed, when you return three days from now."

"I'll not have any doubts at all." He withdrew his hand from her panties and brought it up to his lips to suck the juices off. "I think this is going to be one of the best, don't you, Isabelle? They're both of great quality."

"Yes, I can't wait to get my hands on him, and get underneath that sweet exterior to the man beneath. How are we going to deal with him?" Isabelle asked. "Will you tell him of James and me? Prepare him for a shock when he returns?"

"I think not," said Sebastian. "I had debated doing so – and perhaps taking him round to those Russian twins in the Old Quarter, the ones who have performed so admirably upon other guests of mine in the past. But he is as devoted to young Amanda as she is to him. I don't think it would be wise to give him any inkling of what perhaps might happen at Sandaig Manor before he rejoins his ripe young wife."

"And when you and he return?"

"If you have done your job well, as I know you will, my sweet, we shall have no trouble with Alex. There is Ganfeld's magnificent potion, and the special cigarettes; if he is like so many in the past, he will realise the immense pleasures of the flesh – just as his Amanda surely shall – and become one of us."

"Then we'll proceed along those lines," Isabelle said. "I'll tell James what we've discussed."

"Good," he said, kissing her neck. "Now remember, my love, save some of that fine energy for your husband; don't spend it all on James and Ganfeld – and Genghis, though I refuse to think of you with that –"

"Hush, now," Isabelle cautioned, smiling. "You know that no man satisfies me like you, pet, fat and fiftyish though you may be. Your cock is still the most magnificent I have ever had."

"I could receive no greater compliment, Isabelle, my love."

As they embraced, it was announced that flight IL 377 to Genoa was boarding at Gate 11. All passengers were requested to embark immediately.

Standing several feet away from the venereous, plotting Palermo couple, innocently oblivious of what had been planned for them, the happily married young Americans embraced one last time. Their kiss was long and passionate, and it was with reluctance that Alex Langley withdrew his mouth from the sweet, soft lips of his wife and gently held her away. "They're calling the flight, sweetheart," he said. "Sebastian and I have to board the plane now."

"I know," Amanda said with a sigh. "Oh, Alex, you will be careful, won't you? Please?"

"Of course I will. Now you promised: no worrying."

"Okay."

"We'll be together again soon," he laughed. "After all, what's three little days, anyway?"

Sebastian Palermo, beaming, came up to them just as Amanda was about to reply. "We'd best be getting along, my boy," he said in a kindly voice to Alex. "They're not in the habit of holding flights, even for such important personages as you and me," he winked, poking the younger man lightly on the arm.

Alex laughed, and Amanda managed a smile of her own. Isabelle came up beside her, taking her arm in a friendly way, as the two men stepped through the railed divider, handing their tickets to the man at the raised counter. The man checked the tickets, returned the stubs to them and Alex and Sebastian proceeded down the long corridor that led to the waiting jet. They turned and waved, and Isabelle and Amanda waved back. The young blonde wife blew a kiss to her departing husband just before he was obscured by other passengers.

Amanda sighed a little tremulously. "Oh, Isabelle, I do hope everything will be all right."

"Of course it will, dear," soothed the older, dark-haired woman. "Come along, now. We can watch them take off from the observation deck."

Less than half an hour later, the plane carrying Alex Langley and Sebastian Palermo to Genoa taxied down the runway and executed a routine take-off, being swallowed after a few moments by the thick, grey billows of fog.

"There, you see?" Isabelle chided softly. "Nothing at all to fret about, was there?"

"No, of course not," said Amanda. She made a face. "Sometimes I can be awfully silly."

"Nonsense!" Isabelle replied. "It's perfectly natural to be concerned about the ones you love. I feel the same way about Sebastian flying, even after all these years."

Amanda was surprised. "You do? But you seem so calm."

"A facade, built up over many years," Isabelle said smoothly. "You'll learn the art of being a businessman's wife after a few years, never fear."

"I hope so," said Amanda. "Not only for my sake, but for Alex's."

The two women walked down to the parking area, bending their lithe bodies into the sharp, cold wind which sent the tendrils of fog eddying high overhead. They located the Palermos' Mercedes and slipped inside.

"Brrr," shivered Amanda, hugging herself tightly with both arms; in spite of the heavy clothing she wore, the wind and fog had penetrated to put a chill on her flesh. "I hope it isn't going to be this cold at Sandaig Manor."

"It's forever cold on the hills, Amanda, dear," Isabelle told her, "especially at this time of the year, when the wind starts howling over them. But Sandaig Manor is well-insulated, with central heating; you will feel nothing but warmth and luxury the whole stay, I guarantee."

"Is there a fireplace?" Amanda wanted to know.

"Oh yes, a grand old inglenook. James always keeps a roaring fire going. It's very cosy."

Amanda's enthusiasm for the visit to the baronial home of the wealthy young aristocrat was rapidly returning now that the immediate danger of Alex's leaving had been seen safely through. "I can hardly wait," she said. "From what you've told me about it, it must be really magnificent."

"Oh, it is, it is indeed," Isabelle said. She smiled. "It's like nothing you've ever seen before, dear. I don't think you're going to forget your stay there; I don't think you ever will."

Not if everything goes according to plan, you won't, Isabelle said to herself. And my plans never fail, especially when I have such eager partners as James Figgis and Ganfeld and Genghis, the incomparable...

Isabelle started the expensive car, putting on the heater; moments later, warm air flooded the comfortable interior and quickly dissipated the chill which had overcome Amanda. Once they were out of the airport and on their way, she settled back in complete luxuriousness to enjoy the lengthy drive.

They travelled for the rest of the day, stopping for the night at a small inn near the Scottish border. The next day, they took a brief detour to look at part of Hadrian's wall and arrived at the ferry port of the loch separating them from Sandaig as it began to get dark. The boat, on the instructions of James Figgis, took them to the beginning of the private road that led away to the manor. The sky was dark and overcast, and the wind whistled mournfully at the windows of the sleek Mercedes. Without once consulting a map, Isabelle had navigated her way through increasingly remote country lanes into ever more wild and bleak countryside. She was an excellent driver, and handled the car with ease.

Amanda sat forward expectantly on the seat, peering out through the windscreen. The scenery became more and more sublime. The fog was very thick and wet – Isabelle had had to put the windscreen wipers on, and they made rhythmic little sounds as they swept arcs clear on the glass – but it was high enough so that it did not obliterate the surrounding countryside. Visibility was still very good.

The young blonde wife's impression of the area was that it was bleak and barren and terribly lonely. She had the feeling of having been swallowed up by the hills' vast, rolling emptiness, conveying to her the image of being trapped on some uninhabited wasteland planet far removed from earth. For as far as her eye could see the terrain was covered with low-growing heather and a few stunted, gnarled trees which the fog made ghostly and unreal. Every now and then great stone ruins could be seen – they were ancient, Isabelle explained, perhaps not as old as Stonehenge but antediluvian nonetheless; they were foreboding and cold and lifeless, making Amanda think of things long dead. She shuddered involuntarily, and pulled her coat tighter about her shoulders.

"About the only people who live on these hills, except for semi-recluses with stately old manors like James, are sheep ranchers," Isabelle told her. "They allow the animals to run free over the heather. There – you can see a flock of them off on your left."

Amanda looked, and indeed, several dozen of the thick-wooled animals were grazing in the distance, and further away, she saw a herd of wild ponies huddled together against the damp cold. As she watched them, she saw a small stone structure with a slant roof resembling a shed set back from the narrow, winding road; the front was completely open. "What's that?" she asked, pointing to the structure.

"Shepherd's hutch," Isabelle answered. "Every now and then you'll see a shepherd – usually an old man – sitting inside one of them with his staff."

They proceeded deeper into the hills, and

the desolation seemed to Amanda to become more pronounced. She wasn't so sure now that she liked the idea of spending a week or more – and the first three or four days without Alex – in this godforsaken wilderness. But then, she was probably being silly again; there wasn't anything to worry about. She was among friends, wasn't she?

Suddenly, it seemed to Amanda, two huge, stone cairns, with a massive iron gate heavily padlocked in the centre, blocked the way; high, stone fencing, with spikes rusted and needle-sharp jutting up into the bleak, grey sky, meandered off in both directions from the cairns. Apparently, Amanda thought as Isabelle brought the sedan to a stop in front of the locked gate, James Figgis, or his ancestors, demanded complete privacy for their holdings.

Isabelle took a huge, iron key from the glove compartment and stepped out of the Mercedes. She went to the gate and unlocked the padlock, swinging both halves of the great iron barrier aside. Then she returned to the car, drove through and closed and relocked the gate before continuing on.

The road wandered through the eerie, desolate hills for perhaps a mile or so more and Amanda found herself sitting tense and rigid on the leather seat, peering expectantly through the windscreen for her first glimpse of

Sandaig Manor. It couldn't be very far off, she thought; Isabelle had said that – Suddenly, she saw it.

A small gasp of wonder burst from her ovaled lips, and a delicious chill wound its way along her spine. She had had an idea of what to expect, but actually seeing Sandaig Manor for the first time, through the thin wisps of grey fog that floated ghost-like before it and above it, was an almost shocking experience.

It was a massive, rambling dwelling with gables and turrets and huge, jutting towers that were all but consumed by the trailing vapours of fog; it was fashioned of thick grey-stone blocks upon which ivy and green moss grew in heavy profusion, giving the ancient structure a sinister, awesome air of decaying ruins. Amanda could see stone outbuildings – what had once been, and perhaps still were, servants' quarters – on the left of the manor proper, and high, mossy, stone walls – perhaps enclosing a garden of some type – jutted out sharply to the right. A monstrous wooden door, rounded at the top and set deep into an arch decorated with gargoyles and other hideous stone carvings, sat in the middle of the main front wall, and even at a distance the beautiful blonde wife could see a great, heavy, ornate door-knocker in its centre.

"Quite a sight, isn't it, dear?" Isabelle

asked softly, as she brought the sedan off the access road and onto a wide sweeping drive that circled an immense stone fountain and pond.

"Lord, yes," Amanda whispered, repressing a shiver, her eyes still wide. "All it needs is a moat encircling it to make a medieval castle!"

"James is fond of saying the same thing," chuckled Isabelle. "He says that one of these days he's going to have one dug and filled with alligators."

"Surely he's joking!"

"Oh, of course. James has a wonderful sense of humour, you know."

"He seemed very charming on the two occasions I met him."

"He is, very," Isabelle said. "I think you'll find him a gracious host." Her eyes gleamed brightly, "And he's very eager to please."

There was an area widened out near the wide, stone path leading up to the door, and Isabelle took the Mercedes in there, saying, "James's manservant, Ganfeld, will see to it that the car is put in one of the outbuildings for shelter after the trunk is unpacked."

Amanda nodded, still staring up at the slippery-looking, bare stone walls of the manor house. Well, she thought with a nervous little laugh, I hope the interior is more cheerful than the exterior. But Isabelle said it was very cosy, and I have no reason to doubt her word.

The two women got out of the car, pulling their coats tight around them, and hurried along the path to the door. Amanda saw then that there was a huge plaque in the shape of a shield, which was set into the left side of the arch; it was made of bronze, with the words SANDAIG MANOR in a bas-relief half-circle across the top. Below, there was a depiction of a lion and a great, snarling mastiff and a grim-jawed man in armour plating, forming an interlocking circle by being joined with bunches and clusters of small, round fruit.

Isabelle saw Amanda looking at the plaque and said, "That's the Figgis family crest; quite impressive, isn't it?"

"Oh, yes," replied Amanda. "What does it mean?"

"Well, I'm not sure," Isabelle said, "but I think it has something to do with the ancestral heritage, virility and honour of the Figgises."

"How fascinating!"

"You must have James tell you all about the history of the Figgises," Isabelle urged. "You'll find it intriguing."

"I'll do that," promised the beautiful blonde girl.

When they reached the door, Isabelle raised the heavy, brass knocker, which Amanda saw was in the shape of a huge lion's head with its massive jaws parted, and let it fall. A loud, booming sound echoed eerily through the foggy twilight, and Amanda shivered involuntarily.

They waited for several moments, and then, so suddenly that it startled Amanda and caused her to draw in her breath sharply, the door was pulled open. There, on the threshold, stood a misshapen, deformed little man – a dwarf. He was stooped forward, and Amanda could see that he was a hunchback, in addition to his dwarfism. His face was round and expressionless but his eyes were narrow and beady and seemed to shine with some inner fire. He said in a reedy voice, "Good evening, Mrs Palermo. Is this our guest, Mrs Langley?"

"Yes it is, Ganfeld," answered Isabelle, smiling at the malformed little servant.

The hunchbacked dwarf's eyes seemed to bore right through Amanda's clothing, right through her flesh; they roamed upward along the rich curves of her fine young body, paused on her face and then skittered away to fasten on Isabelle again. Amanda repressed a shudder at the ugly little man's scrutiny of her; Isabelle could have at least warned her, she thought, that James's manservant was a dwarf – and a hunchback on top of that.

"Won't you come inside?" Ganfeld said to them. "The master is waiting in the library.

He expected you'd be here about this time."

"Thank you, Ganfeld."

The dwarf, who was dressed in butler's livery, led them down a long, dark corridor, hung with tapestries and medieval fighting equipment such as maces, broadswords and crossbows. Following, Amanda felt an added twinge of pity and discomfort to find that the little man was not only hunchbacked, but club footed as well; his right leg made sharp, staccato thumping sounds on the stone-flagged floor of the corridor.

Ganfeld opened a set of huge, ornately carved wooden doors and ushered them into an immense, high-ceilinged room with bookshelves lining two of the four walls, the largest fireplace Amanda had ever seen taking up an entire third and beautiful tapestries decorating a fourth. The furnishings were old and heavy and comfortable-looking, of dark wood and leather. An impressive bar reposed diagonally across the corner between one wall of bookshelves and the tapestried one and, as the two women entered, a tall, smiling man with wavy, salt-and-pepper hair and classic features came toward them with his hands outstretched.

He wore a wine-coloured velvet smoking jacket, a flowered cravat, and dove-grey slacks; on his feet were expensive doe-skin moccasins. He was about forty and very handsome, with a small, neatly-clipped moustache, and Amanda couldn't help but notice the graceful, fluid way he moved as he approached them. He was a very virile-looking man, and his dark eyes reflected his masculinity as well as warmth and good humour.

"Isabelle, Mrs Langley!" he greeted them in his deep, resonant voice. "So good to see you! Did you get the men off to Genoa on schedule?"

"We certainly did, James," Isabelle told him.

"You're looking lovely tonight, my dear," he told her, kissing her warmly on the cheek. He turned to Amanda and took her hands in his. "And so are you, my dear Mrs Langley. You're positively radiant."

Amanda felt herself blushing appreciatively. "Why, thank you, James!" she said, pleased at the compliment.

He smiled disarmingly, taking both women by the hand. He led them toward the massive inglenook fireplace, where a roaring wood fire cast flickering shadows and welcome warmth into the remainder of the room. "You must be tired and cold, after your long drive from London," Figgis said. "Would you like a brandy before you go to your rooms? It will take Ganfeld a few minutes to transfer your bags from the car upstairs, anyway."

"A brandy would be lovely, James," said Isabelle.

"Yes, thank you," agreed Amanda.

They sat by the fire, drinking brandy and talking of small things. Amanda found herself relaxing immediately, her discomfort about the hills and the foreboding exterior of Sandaig Manor – and the disconcerting sight of the malformed dwarf Ganfeld – melting into warm relaxation with the brandy and the fire. The library was lovely, just as Isabelle had said it would be, and James was handsome, gracious and concerned. If the rest of Sandaig Manor turned out to be as fascinating as the corridor with its tapestries and medieval weapons and the library with its wonderful fireplace and cosy atmosphere, then she was really going to enjoy her stay here immensely. She could spend the whole time inside the stately grounds, and leave the exploration of the hills to the time when Alex came three or four days hence.

A half-hour passed, during which time James told Amanda she had the complete run of the manor; she could explore the building and grounds at her leisure, or take a guided tour with him or Ganfeld. The young blonde wife, thinking of the pitiable dwarf, told him that she would probably do it on her own, but that she would likely be besieging him with questions about this and that. Figgis laughed, telling her that he was there to serve her, and that she had only to ask in order to receive.

Ganfeld entered the library shortly thereafter and announced that the ladies' rooms were ready. James said that they would be having dinner around eight, a little more than an hour hence, which would give them plenty of time to freshen up and change.

Ganfeld led them up a marble staircase to the second floor. Amanda took the opportunity to whisper to Isabelle, "Shall I dress formally for dinner?"

"I think it would be appropriate this first night," Isabelle told her.

"All right."

Amanda's room turned out to be sumptuously appointed, with a private bath. There was a great double bed with antique headboard and frame, a huge antique wardrobe and several other pieces of furniture. Her bags had been placed on the carpet next to the bed.

When she had been left alone, the young blonde wife undressed leisurely and drew a hot bath in the ornate and old-fashioned leg tub. Then she slipped into the soothing water and closed her eyes, letting its warmth envelop her.

Yes, she thought drowsily as she soaked, this is going to be a wonderful vacation after all, even though Alex will only be able to spend part of it with me. I have a feeling that Isabelle was right in what she said in the car; I don't think I am going to forget these next few days at Sandaig Manor.

Chapter 2

Amanda was overwhelmed by the dinner. The fine silver, the white bone china plates with the gold rims, the candelabras at either end of the long oak table...

She had never seen such sumptuousness, nor such food, nor such service, and she felt ill at ease. While James and Isabelle carried on a witty conversation and sparkling rejoinders back and forth all through the five courses, Amanda kept to herself, only speaking when spoken to, nodding and smiling at other times, and worrying about the sleeves of her blue organdie dinner dress when she wasn't eating.

The blue organdie was a bad choice, a mistake she instantly realised when entering the dining room, after having descended the broad, banistered stairs from the second floor. She didn't have the proper clothes for such an affair to begin with; being American and the wife of a still rising businessman, she didn't attend affairs of this calibre. The blue organdie was formal, but didn't have the polish or sophistication that, say, the black lace Empire dress Isabelle was wearing possessed. The quiet, dignified grace just wasn't there – it made her seem young, like a pubescent girl going to her junior prom. She was, in brief, embarrassed.

Ganfeld, impeccable in his black uniform, served and cleared with a subservience almost touching. It was obvious to Amanda that the little hunchback doted on his master, lived and breathed to serve James Figgis, to repay the debt of gratitude for being employed as a respectable man rather than a sideshow freak. Ganfeld hobbled around at amazing speed, his miniature club foot with its built-up shoe thumping against the thick Oriental carpeting with the rapidity of a jackhammer. He had to reach up to the table for the dishes and glasses, but in spite of his infirmities not a dish clattered, nor a glass pinged.

Amanda watched Ganfeld, torn between her ambivalent feelings of repulsion and of pity. There was a sort of horror to the dwarf, a kind of wolfish glitter to his eyes and an evil smirk to his rubbery lips which, when he faced Amanda, made her cringe. It was – well, it was almost as if he was undressing her with his eyes, leering at her as though envisioning her stripped completely naked in bed! A cold, clammy shiver would travel the length of her spine, then, and her stomach would grow queasy.

And yet that couldn't be, she told herself. It was her imagination; it had to be. Ganfeld had been nothing save the beautifully trained gentleman's gentleman that he was, acting as butler, servant and chef with aplomb. And always with proper manners. Not once had he spoken out of turn or made any untoward gesture to her, and he had treated her with the respect and deference that she, as a house-guest of his master, should be afforded. So Amanda felt guilty, concluding that her unwarranted fear of Ganfeld was nothing more than prejudice and aversion to his unfortunate plight.

Ganfeld could not help what he was. It was an accident of birth, she kept reminding herself, a tragedy of sperm and ovum that was a curse to him, and one which he must surely know caused contempt and revulsion on the part of other, more normal humans. She was being unfair and as ugly in her mind as he was on the surface, she thought, and therefore she felt sorry for him as well. "The slings and arrows of outrageous fortune," she quoted in her mind. She watched Ganfeld, then; watched him with the fascination with which humanity watches all great sorrows.

Poor girl. Had she but known what was burning through the hunchbacked dwarf's mind, she wouldn't have been so full of self-chastisement. Ganfeld went through the motions of servitude, starting from the first answering of the door, through the carrying of her bags upstairs to the guest bedroom and the serving of dinner with but one licentious flame lusting in the furnace of his sadistic brain. Soon... soon I will possess this proud beauty, this American bitch who looks at me with such coldness... yes, soon I will have her, and she'll like it. She'll love it, love me, me and my fine, huge cock worming around in her proud young belly. Soon...

The last course had been served, the dessert of Camembert cheese and ripe fruit. The last of the knives and forks which had lined each side of the place settings had been used to cut and eat, the china plates with the pits and seeds had been removed and there was a long pause as the three of them sat back, touched their mouths with the linen napkins and slothfully contemplated the large amounts they'd just consumed.

"Shall we have coffee now?" Isabelle asked.

"Ah, yes," James replied, smiling. "Ganfeld!"

"Coming," Ganfeld said from the kitchen, and then he appeared. "You wish for coffee?"

"In the living room, I think. And a little

Grand Marnier, perhaps." James rose, placing his napkin on the table, and smiled at both Isabelle and Amanda. "I think we'll be more comfortable there, don't you agree?"

"I'm not sure I can move," Amanda said. "I'm so full." There had been soup, a fine clear broth sprinkled with chives and parsley, then the fish course. Amanda had never been one for fish, but the little fried surf-fish were in a mixture of lemon juice and butter and melted in her mouth. Fresh, James had assured her, caught just that morning. And then the fillets, the eye of the beef broiled with garlic and the hearts of artichokes, and the side course of snow peas and the baked potato still in its jacket, bursting with sour cream. And, of course, the final course of fruit. Never had she eaten so much or so well, and her dress was tight around her expanded stomach.

Somehow she made it to the library and was nearly in a stupor, almost uncomfortable, and she couldn't understand how her host could keep such a trim, muscular figure if he ate like that every day. Or, for that matter, how James and Isabelle could still carry on their spirited discussion, have so much energy for other things besides digestion.

James was expounding. "I cannot agree that the change in our government is for the better."

"But you yourself said, my dear James, that you weren't for the Liberals or for Labour," Isabelle replied. "I would think that you'd be all for the Conservatives to be back in power."

"That's just it," James replied. "They aren't in power. Oh, they were voted in, Edward Heath to the Prime Minister's chair and all, but it doesn't make one whit of difference. Not one whit."

"Why?" Amanda asked simply. She had never delved into politics much; as an American she didn't feel that she should form opinions about English politics, and she had left most of the domestic politics to her husband. Still, what James was saying puzzled her.

"Because the government doesn't hold the reins of power, Mrs Langley. May I call you Amanda?"

"Of course; please do, Mr Figgis," she blushed. "I mean James."

He smiled at her slip and continued. "Now in answer to your question, you must understand that in any important nation – yours, mine, Russia, France, whatever – you have a bureaucracy, a grey, anonymous world of officialdom, a growing army of civil servants, council officials, tax inspectors and big business administrators. It is, as Balzac said, 'a giant mechanism operated by pygmies'."

"Naturally, there's the staff. But –" Amanda was interrupted by Ganfeld bearing a shiny silver tray of coffee and cups and liqueur and glasses. Ganfeld set the tray down and proceeded to pour and serve. Amanda continued. "But they are controlled by the government."

"On the contrary. Ah, thank you, Ganfeld." James stirred his coffee. "It's the other way around. Consider: the incoming party have been denied information on which to base political decisions because they were formally the opposition. Without such information, all their big talk about changing ways is irrelevant."

"But they have the information when they are in power," Amanda protested. She sipped her Grand Marnier tentatively, enjoying its combination of sweet stickiness and bitter fruit flavour.

"That's it, Amanda, Grand Marnier is an excellent digestive aid. I always follow my evening meal with it." James turned to Ganfeld, who had finished serving. "My Partagas, Ganfeld, if you please. And the, ah, special cigarettes." Then he turned back to the beautiful young wife. "I'm sorry for the interruption, Amanda," he sighed. "No, I'm afraid they don't have the information. The only way a minister could effectively challenge an already existing policy would be by going into the whole thing again from scratch, reading all the papers, tracing all the details of planning and contracting from the moment the project was conceived to the stage at which it arrived on his desk claiming an urgent decision. And that is exactly what he can't do. He has neither the time nor the specialist knowledge. He is forced to take most of what has gone before as read."

Again the conversation was interrupted by the hunchbacked servant, who this time appeared with a large wooden box and a smaller silver one. He opened the silver box and offered its contents to Isabelle; Amanda could see slightly that the interior was of scarlet velvet and the contents a brownish type of cigarette. Isabelle took one and Ganfeld bent forward and lit the oddly coloured cigarette with a large butane gas lighter of the same design as the silver box.

"The minister," James went on to say, "as well as the whole new government are limited by ignorance, in other words."

"Then how can decisions be made?" Amanda asked. The box was passed to her. "Oh, no, thank you, Ganfeld. I prefer my own brand."

"No, do take one my dear," James urged. "They're something special, a grade of foreign tobacco much better than our English Virginia which yours are no doubt made of. I insist;

it's as much an after-dinner ritual at Sandaig Manor as Grand Marnier, or my Cuban cigars."

Amanda selected one, feeling its coarse paper in her fingers as she put its cork-wrapped tip in her mouth. Ganfeld applied the fire; she inhaled. It was strange, an entirely different kind of taste than her brand – an odd, sour-sweet flavour which seemed to go deeper in her lungs, imbibing an entirely new sensation than she had ever experienced while smoking since... since she first began! She inhaled again, smelling the pungency of the tobacco. It wasn't rough, like a coarse American cigarette might be, just edifying, giving her that same euphoria as had happened when she had snuck a Camel from her father's package and smoked it secretly behind the garage many years ago. A simple matter of getting used to, she supposed.

"Certainly strong," she commented, blinking.

James had clipped the end of the Partagas cigar, which he had selected from the large wooden humidor Ganfeld had brought to him. "Yes, aren't they? Very tasty, I'd say. A mixture of Latakia, Turkish, Burley and cannabis," he winked knowingly at Isabelle, who seemed to have a silly smirk on her face as though she was sharing some kind of secret with him. "Mostly the latter," he added.

"Can – cana –?" she tried to pronounce the last named tobacco. Somehow she was having a hard time focusing her mind on the word; things were getting a little woozy, in fact.

"Cannabis," James repeated. "Sometimes referred to as *grifti*, when it comes from Morocco as this particular batch did."

"Oh." It really didn't seem to matter. She continued to smoke, letting the lethargy she felt after the meal, the liqueur and, peculiarly, the cigarette, take over her body.

"To get back to what I was saying," James continued, "the information the minister receives has been filtered many times by whom? By the same bureaucracy, by the same civil servants who have been there before him, before his predecessor, no doubt. The minister has no way of knowing what was discarded, what was emphasised. He may think he has a choice of three or four courses of action, but each of those courses has been plotted by his top civil servants, and they leave him little doubt about which course they think to be the best. Theoretically the minister is in power, is free to reject that advice, but the fact is that he must always be dependent."

"That's a very cynical approach, James," Isabelle was saying.

To Amanda, her hearing was fading, for

Isabelle seemed to be further away, as if speaking from the end of some long, narrow, echoing hall. She frowned and shook her head, trying to clear her mind, but it didn't seem to do any good. Moreover, she didn't really care. Everything was too pleasant, too relaxing to get excited over. She sank still further into the feather-like softness of the couch and kicked off her shoes. Yes, it was too much trouble to keep up the pretence of correctness – she hiked her stockinged feet up and tucked them under her buttocks. Her dress bunched around her waist... she should pull it down, stay modest, if informal, but again, it was too much trouble. So much nicer just to stay as she was and drink her Grand Marnier and smoke the odd cigarette with the Moroccan *grifti*.

"Not cynical, Isabelle," James replied. "Just practical."

"Practical," Amanda repeated soporifically. She thought the word was fun and tripped it lightly over her tongue a few times, even humming a little tune along with it. There was a small, faint warning in the back of her head, saying: what's wrong? Why are you acting like this? But she didn't pay any heed to it. The room was so beautiful, more beautiful than she had realised, so full of colours, and that tapestry hanging over the credenza seemed almost alive with hues and shades. She stared at the tapestry, soaking in every detail and thread of its woven hunter-and-stag design.

"Practical," Isabelle was saying from far, far away. "Practical like smoking marijuana, James?"

Marijuana... that was bad... very naughty to smoke marijuana... did things to people. Amanda smiled at Isabelle vaguely, not once relating the reference to the drug to her own condition.

"I'm always practical, my love," James said. "That way I get what I want."

"You always get what you want, don't you?" Isabelle stood up and crossed to the wide leather chair in which James was seated. She seemed to take a century to walk to him, or so Amanda thought; such a slow walker... and now what was she doing? Leaning over, also in slow motion, I can see her lips puckered as though she were going to kiss him... how nice... kissing is a sign of love... I kiss Alex all the time... I'd like to have Alex with me right now, to kiss me hard as James is kissing Isabelle, to fondle my breasts as he is...

"And you want her, don't you?" Isabelle asked, nibbling his ear. "You want to fuck her as you have fucked me and all the other girls, don't you?"

Fuck... fuck, that's a bad word, isn't it? Fuck, fuck... mustn't use the word fuck. Why is Isabelle using the word fuck? Who is this other "her" that she is talking about? Amanda saw then that Ganfeld was bending over her, his wicked grin making his face a contorted mask of lechery. She allowed him to remove the stub of the cigarette from her fingers, place another tube of cannabis – of marijuana – in her mouth and light it. She sucked in the smoke as he refilled her liqueur glass.

"To my mind," James said, "the only thing wrong with the system is that we pretend that the civil servants, that the bureaucracy, aren't running the show. I think that they should be recognised for what they are – professional managers."

James Figgis seemed to be talking to Isabelle, to continue explaining about the true happenings behind the scenes at Whitehall, to be exposing the workings of the inner circle of the British government – of, in actuality, any elective government. What he had to say was as important to understanding Washington, DC as it was to the Conservative government in England, and perhaps at another time, another place, it would have been appreciated for the insight that it was.

But Figgis was continuing for other reasons. His eyes were beadily fixed on the ever more drugged young American wife near him, greedily watching her as she fell more and more under the hypnotic powers of the potent cigarettes... Yes, he wanted to fuck her something fierce... his penis and testicles ached to slip inside the tender, palpitating cunt of the innocent beauty and spew his hot, white seed deep, deep inside her proud womb. That, and other more intensely exciting defilements of her body and soul. And Isabelle would help him, he knew, just as she always had, for she got tremendous enjoyment out of bringing lovely, haughty young wives to their knees and seeing their helpless subjugation, their eventual change into debauched women of the flesh, and her own joining in the fun and games.

All in good time, he realised, for he was, as the harlot wife of his best friend, Sebastian Palermo, had said, a totally practical man. Planning, that was the key, and so he droned on, making sure that Amanda Langley was lulled into an unguarded position in which it would be easier to strike her.

He droned on, and all the while he had his hand up the frilly dress of the black-haired wife sitting in his lap. His fingers teased the inside of her creamy thighs, making them quiver, then his fingers tickled around the gusset of her panties, feeling the outline of her fleshy, palpitating pussy, the wetness of her lubricious, excited state, the curly hairs of her pubic mound as they peeked out of the sides of her panties and grazed his hand.

"In short," he was saying, his mind delving

into the fun which he would have in a few more minutes when he would fuck the older of the two women to within an inch of her life, conjuring the image of her firm, yielding flesh cemented to his hard, muscled body and the look of glazed enrapturement in her eyes as she cried out her passion. "In short, the healthiest thing would be to cast out the fiction. Let the politicians remain responsible for the broadest policy, and let the permanent officials come out from behind their bushes and be ready to undertake public accounting for their management of our affairs."

"Ohh... ohh... ohh..." breathed the now trembling black-haired female in his clasp. "Ohh... I want you to fuck me, James... take me like some rutting beast of the fields... give it to me... ohh..." She surged against his wandering fingers, which were now insinuated inside her panties and sliding into the slippery, pink vaginal opening of her cunt. "Uhhh..."

"But, alas, I see no sign of it happening." James still had his eyes feasted on Amanda Langley, the naïve wife who would never return to her old ways after the stay at his mansion, and he saw that the marijuana had now taken its fullest effect. She was sprawled most unladylike on the sofa, her legs dangling and her dress nearly up to her hips. He could see up her legs, up to the little wisp of flimsy white nylon that separated him from his goal of her tender young pussy. It excited him, and his cock leaped into total erection, hurting to be released from the prison of his pants.

"I think she's ready," he said to Isabelle.

"Ohhh... I am... I ammm too." Isabelle Palermo was panting now, openly spreading her legs to his searching hand.

"Then let's get started. Right here, right in front of her. She's so doped up that she won't be horrified; only excited," James chuckled obscenely, pulling his fingers from the older woman's vagina with a slightly wet sluicing sound. "Get up, my love. Get up and take your clothes off. I want to fuck you right here, right on the rug, right in front of Little Miss Sweetness. Hah! Let's see just how much of a goody-goody she is after she gets a taste of voyeurism, eh?"

The room was spinning for the beautiful young wife, Amanda Langley. She had been drunk before, her surroundings revolving as if she were on a carousel; but it wasn't like that this time. No, it was as if the colours and the objects were made of some pliable rubber which would alter and vary shape, size and texture at will. A kaleidoscope of patterns which were dizzying and satisfying both, and gave new and deep meaning to the everyday items that they were. Amanda didn't understand what had taken over her mind, her body... but she didn't care. Nothing mattered except the song in her ears, the sight before her eyes and the sweet pungency of the cigarette between her lips.

But what were James and Isabelle doing? Where were they? She tried to concentrate on the two people. They were... were on the rug! And, and it seemed as though they were naked! Amanda shook her head again, her blonde hair whipping around, unable to believe what she was seeing. No... She clenched her eyes tightly together, then opened them wide. They were still there... and they were... OH MY GOD! Amanda's heart skipped a beat.

Isabelle was lying spreadeagled before the fireplace, completely nude. Amanda felt as though she could have reached out and touched her. Isabelle's head was rolling back and forth, her face contorted with ecstasy. James was kneeling between her naked widespread legs, running his tongue moistly up and down her body. Isabelle writhed beneath his flickering caresses like a woman possessed, her hands tangling tightly in his hair, pulling his lips greedily to her tingling skin.

Amanda gripped the corners of the cushion, leaning forward. Isabelle... and James! She tried to blot out the shocking picture, but she couldn't. She had to look – the obscene spectacle mesmerised her. Her mind rebelled at the sight of a man toying with the naked, squirming body of a woman who was the wife of your own husband's boss... she knew she should turn away. But she couldn't. She couldn't move!

Amanda sucked harder, as if hypnotised on the brown cigarette, the conscience-killing smoke sweeping away the revulsion, lightening her head. Then, after a few, deep inhalations, she found herself wickedly enjoying the scene before her; watching with studied detachment the pagan ritual that was as old as time itself.

Isabelle was beautiful, she thought, as she gazed in intoxicated rapture at the enchanting woman spread on the floor. James had worked her to a fever pitch and the older woman's mouth hung open in ecstasy. James Figgis's face was just above her softly curling pubic mound, his hands pressed on the smooth, flat plane of her stomach and his thumbs pressed into the fleshy outer flanges of her cunt-lips, pulling outward, exposing the moist, red slit of the woman's vagina. The dainty pink bud of her clitoris was clearly visible, throbbing into hardness just above the stretched elastic opening of her vaginal tunnel.

James's head dropped and his long, wet tongue snaked out to flick at the quivering little nub of raw nerves. Mrs Palermo's body jerked as the electric contact was made and her legs clamped tightly around his head, her soft inner thighs imprisoning his ears in a vice-like grip. Her hips began to rotate and soft wails of animal pleasure escaped from her mouth.

The innocent blonde wife on the couch gaped in disbelief as she watched her husband's boss's wife's lustful twistings to the depraved mouthing of her loins. She drew deeper on her marijuana cigarette, feeling her mind opening like a budding flower, uncertain any more whether the two writhing figures on the floor were real or figments of her imagination. Time was dancing in her head, and nothing existed in the world except the couple before her – and somehow she felt mystically connected with them.

Amanda's own torso began an involuntary swaying in time to that of Isabelle, and the thin folds of her dress and panties grated against her tiny, sensitive anus and vagina, sending spasms of pleasure rippling through her loins and belly and on up to the rising nipples of her breasts.

And then James extricated himself from the now mewling, mindless black-haired woman on the floor, and he gazed down from his kneeling position at the wife of his friend, his mouth and lips wet from his saliva and her vaginal secretions. He was panting from his own excitement – Amanda could hear his ragged breaths – and he stroked his hard penis which jutted from his thighs.

Amanda Langley, who had never had or seen any other man except her own husband, paled and sucked in her breath at the sight of James's cock. She sat immobile, much of the nirvana that the drug had caused ripped from her as cold air can revive a drunk. She watched in terrified fascination as James's fingers skinned the thick foreskin rapidly up and down the full length, the hardened head bursting momentarily into view each time like a giant monster crawling from its secret lair. She was so close that she could see the glistening seminal fluid oozing forth from it. James's hoarse breathing made it quiver, and right then, his penis seemed to the frightened young wife the most monstrous thing in the world. She could not imagine ever having something like that inside her. No woman could take it! It would kill her!

And then Isabelle reached up and grabbed James, and James lunged – and without hesitation, his gleaming, rock-hard cock plunged into her moist, open vagina. He immediately began to fuck Palermo's wife with long, hard strokes, and Amanda could clearly see his shaft sliding in and out of her friend's pink widespread cunt like a well-oiled piston, his sperm-laden balls smacking rhythmically into the moist crevice of her wide-splayed buttocks below.

Amanda waited for Isabelle to scream in protest, or to fight back against the obscene rape of her open vagina – but none came. Instead, her older girl friend's legs quivered momentarily up in the air and then snaked back python-like around his waist. Her hands slid slowly down his gleaming body and came to rest on his white, hollowing buttocks. The fingers spread, whitened from pressure, then pulled him gluttonously into her, while below, the softly clenching lips of her cunt flowered open in acceptance. It swallowed the whole of his plunging cock with each surging heave, and small piteous pleas of passionate supplication began to roll from her lips. They were lewd and filthy supplications, using words which Amanda had seldom heard except in whispers from the more daring girls back in college.

Amanda held her breath, more of the marijuana-induced veil being lifted from her hazed, unbelieving eyes, and though she sat there as if glued, her hands over her wide-open mouth in horror, her mind was now beginning to snap out of its lethargy enough for her to grasp firmly the total salaciousness of the situation. The act was alien to her and her own sheltered life, the absolute nadir of every moral code to which the young naïve wife had ever subscribed.

Isabelle's buttocks were grinding ever

faster now, and her groans and mewls of pleasure were becoming more desperate. The demonic couplings were met with equal fury by James as he fucked harder and harder into her, driving her buttocks flat to the rug with each lust-inspired surge. The loud slap of their naked bellies against each other resounded in Amanda's fevered head like claps of thunder. The drugged girl stayed in her seat as though hypnotised by the curling and uncurling legs as her girl friend strove in final desperation to reach her completion.

Amanda couldn't stand any more! Her heart and soul were in turmoil with revulsion and excitement, with horror and lewd interest, with unbelief and realisation, with the shock of reality and the lulling of the drug. Something had to give!

Suddenly from Isabelle came a low, unearthly howl, and her hotly grinding buttocks quivered and jerked up tight against the hardened penis sunk deep in her cunt. James groaned above her and ground down hard, his thick fleshy rod throbbing its white, milky sperm deep up into her widening belly. The rich fluid filled her to overflowing and cascaded warmly out around her pink, moist vaginal lips. To Amanda's horror, she could see clearly a tiny, white stream of it wetly trickling down the wide-split crevice of her buttocks and onto the Oriental rug. The couple spasmed, endlessly expending their mindless orgasms as though she, a guest in the house, did not even exist!

The loud cry, the sight of another man's seed spilling so wantonly upon the carpet – the final link had been broken, and Amanda was released from her subjective bondage on the couch. No longer did the drug or the shock of seeing her friend, another man's wife, copulate openly before her with a strange man fascinate her to immobility. Everything was shattered. She leaped up and stumbled blindly toward the hall. Tears of abject humiliation rolled down her cheeks, smearing the light coat of make-up she'd applied before going to dinner. She ran up the stairs, not knowing where to go, where to hide, where to find an avenue of escape.

There was none. She was stuck in a house of sin and devilry, a captive of the immense, silent, deadly hills with no means of crossing them on her own. She couldn't leave... but she couldn't stay. Not now!

Oh God, what could she do? She flung herself down the upstairs hall toward the only sanctuary she knew, the only place even remotely familiar and comforting – her guest room.

Chapter 3

The door-knob turned. Ganfeld, the hunchbacked dwarf, became immediately attentive in his hiding place inside the huge antique wardrobe in Amanda Langley's room. He manoeuvred his deformed body so that one eye was pressed to the small hole that had inconspicuously been bored in the left-hand door, his muscles tensed with barely repressed excitement.

The light snapped on overhead and he could see the lithe, voluptuous blonde wife as she ran across the room and flung herself on the bed. She began weeping unabashedly, her lovely face twisted with emotion. Ganfeld smiled tightly, pressing his eye hard against the hole; he could tell by the brightness of her eyes and the flushed appearance of her cheeks that the marijuana that she had partaken of had done its job well. And he thought he knew, too, why she was weeping; his master always became uncontrollably horny when he smoked pot, and James had likely taken the insatiable Isabelle somewhere for a satisfying fuck – somewhere not too far removed from the naïve young eyes of the beautiful Amanda Langley.

Yes, Ganfeld was sure that was why Amanda

was crying. She wouldn't have expected to see her friend Isabelle so abandonedly spreading her legs for Figgis, and in her semi-drugged condition she had probably fled in humiliation to her room. Good, good, thought the grinning dwarf. Everything was working out exactly as they had planned...

After a time Amanda raised herself on the bed and dried her eyes. She heaved a shuddering sigh and got tremulously to her feet. The little hunchback watched hungrily as she began to undress, slipping out of her organdie dress and removing her sheer panties and brassiere until she stood naked for a moment in the bright light overhead. Ganfeld sucked in his breath, small beads of perspiration breaking out on his forehead, as his watching eye feasted on the dark, soft silkiness that covered the junction of her perfectly formed legs, the thin, red, hair-lined slit that was temptingly visible running the full length of her pubic triangle, the alabaster contours of her hips and the white, rounded spheres of her breasts with their pink little nipples turgid from her agitated mental state. His mouth watered. He could hardly wait to get his hands and mouth on those tempting buds, to twist and churn them into the rock-hardness of helpless passion.

As he watched, Amanda took a thin, diaphanous nightgown from her suitcase and slipped it over her nakedness with the sibilant rustling of silk. Then she sat down on the bed, sighing once more. Ganfeld held his breath again, willing her to look at the bedside table, to see the bottle of sherry and the glass he had placed there before entering the wardrobe to hide. Come on, my little beauty, the salivating dwarf thought. It's for you, all for you. A little potion which will set that lovely little pussy of yours twitching, as it has set so many pussies twitching in the past. A maddeningly irresistible aphrodisiac mixed with the sherry, and all for you...

As if her mind somehow read and interpreted the evil little hunchback's thoughts, Amanda's eyes swivelled to the night-stand and rested on the bottle of sherry. Obediently, she reached out a hand and closed it around the bottle, raised it and poured some of the ruby liquid into the glass. She needed a drink, she thought in her half-drugged mind, something to steady her nerves after the terrible, unnerving scene she had witnessed downstairs – something to make her sleep, sleep away the images of the naked entwined bodies of James and Isabelle which seemed burned indelibly on the retinas of her eyes.

Ganfeld smiled in anticipation when he saw her lift the glass of sherry to her lips and drink deeply from it. She drank again and then lay back on the bed, reaching up to switch off the light and send the room into semi-darkness. It took Ganfeld's eyes a moment to adjust to the change but he could still see her slim form stretched sensuously down the length of the bed. He clenched his fist tightly as she squirmed around before him, trying to get comfortable; he'd show this proud little American bitch who had everything and who had looked so pityingly at him. He would really show her! But he had to be patient, had to wait a few more minutes. He wanted no crying out; the potion had to have time to reach its full effect. His body was soaked in sweat now from the thought of that haughty young bitch squirming in helpless surrender beneath his hardened, oversized cock. The seconds of waiting ticking by seemed like hours – and finally he could stand it no longer. His cock throbbed achingly in his pants; he had to have her, on his terms, right this moment!

He opened the wardrobe door slowly, pushing his head into the semi-darkened room. There was no sound but the soft breathing of the now completely motionless young wife on the bed. He closed the door softly, peering intensely through the darkness at the bed. The head of the sleeping girl was facing straight ahead at the ceiling, and her eyes were clenched tightly shut as if in a deep, hard sleep – yet she moved slightly from time to time as though dreams were coming to her from the haze of a nether-world.

The dwarf, dragging his club foot, moved cat-like around the foot of the bed, not taking his gaze from the reclining figure sprawled there. Amanda had drawn one knee up flat on the bed even with her hip, the smooth, white flesh of her soft inner thigh gleaming faintly in the darkness where the gown had pulled up in her restlessness. The soft, dark hairs covering the exposed, still slightly closed lips of her vagina were plainly visible now to his beady eyes.

He involuntarily drew in his breath at the unbelievable sight before him. He had fucked many drugged young women in the home of his master, James Figgis, but never any like this! Never any so pure, innocent and proud; never any that he would enjoy humiliating so much.

The thought of helpless, mewling grunts of pleasure coming from those untouchable lips that had scorned and pitied him before, goaded his already half-erect prick into granite hardness. He could feel the blood throbbing painfully into its large, expanded head, tiny droplets of thick, white seminal fluid already beginning to seep from the sensitive contracting gland to smear wetly against his thigh.

He silently opened the fly of his trousers, easing the pain slightly.

Slowly, Ganfeld massaged the heavy, thick foreskin back and forth over the jerking head of his huge, disproportionately thick cock, a member he was sadistically proud of, his only claim to power and masculinity. Many a woman had cowered before the monster in the past, and many more would cower so in the future; he might have been a dwarf, a hunchback, but the huge, throbbing prick which he now massaged in his gnarled fingers was indeed his equaliser; it gave him all the stature he needed in the world.

Now he advanced toward the proud young bitch who lay totally at his mercy. The marijuana and the aphrodisiac had done their work well indeed, and he now intended to teach this haughty young American wife a lesson she'd never forget. This rod which he would ram deep, deep between those open thighs would teach her and her kind to treat him like he was a pitiable sideshow freak!

Ganfeld's pants dropped heavily to the floor as he opened the last button at the top and fully exposed his long, thick member. It stood out in proud, menacing erection over the spreadeagled body on the bed beneath. He removed the rest of his clothes, then, and stood for a moment longer hunched over the motionless flesh, stroking himself into a rigidity that threatened to explode into streaming, white-hot spurts at any moment. For a second he considered it. It would be a beautiful sight to see his hard penis throbbing out its load into the helpless young wife's face and down over her soft, white tits. He lewdly pictured it dribbling down over her chin to the hollow of her throat and forming warm, sticky pools between those lush, quivering breasts. But no, he had better plans for her tonight, plans which would be the major first step in this beautiful woman's total debauchery.

Still, he couldn't resist one thing before he continued according to plan. He knew the risk was great of losing his load, but he had to see those little ruby lips around his cock just for a moment. He had thought so much about it while he was waiting in the wardrobe for her to come upstairs. He swung his dwarf body up on the edge of the bed by her head and turned it gently toward his erected member. When it was several inches away, he pushed his hips slowly forward toward her upturned face, laying the wet, sticky underside of the palpitating head between the small valley formed by her closed, lipstick-covered lips. He placed one thumb under her nose and the other on her chin, pulling slowly out until the underside of the heavy head dropped slightly through the stretched lips and rested against her white teeth, the soft flesh of the pink, puckered lips forming a furrow along its length. He flexed his hips slightly back and forth until several small droplets of come flowed from his throbbing gland, and lubricated the mouth that was half surrounding it. He could feel the warm air from her nostrils pushing hotly against it as she breathed in and out restlessly.

Looking down directly into her face, he could see small rivulets run slowly down the corners of her mouth on either side, dribbling like tears down the sides of her cheeks. Goddamn, he would like to shoot his hot, boiling semen down that soft, trembling throat and see her Adam's apple bob up and down as she gulped it on into her belly. Maybe later on during her stay he would have that opportunity; he couldn't be greedy now.

The deformed hunchback reached one hand down to the hem of the flimsy negligee, pulling it up slowly over the young wife's rounded, snow-white belly, over the large, globular breasts, until her whole naked body was exposed. He had seen it through the hole in the wardrobe while watching her undress, but it hadn't excited him nearly as much as having it here now, spread helplessly beneath him, where he could touch and fondle it at his whim.

He used the thumb and forefinger of his right hand to push her lips tighter against the purple-veined cock between them, gently continuing the slow, sawing motion of his hips. The other hand moved over the magnificent breasts, tweaking the nipples until he could feel them mechanically hardening under his manipulations.

Amanda Langley shifted slightly beneath him, moaning softly as though aware of his presence. He held still and his rod fell from between her loose lips down over her chin, leaving thin threads of warm, white stickiness trailing behind it.

"Alex, Alex, darling," she mumbled thickly through the fog of the drug. "Come to me, my darling husband... I want you..."

Ganfeld smiled to himself above her. So, he thought, the bitch thinks I'm her husband, eh? He chuckled lewdly to himself. Well, she'll see the difference before I'm finished, and no mistake!

He stroked the giant, throbbing cock slowly, reaching down and running his other hand over the awakening mounds of her tits and down over her belly to the soft, fleshy folds of her cunt.

"Ooohhh, Alex, lover," Amanda moaned, dreaming that her beloved husband was near her, about to make love to her, her body becoming alert now to the caresses of the magic hands that were stroking her flesh into a hot sheet of desire. God, how she wanted him now, wanted Alex, and her body ached with her rising aphrodisiac-induced need to be touched as he was touching her this very moment.

Her tongue ran slowly around her moist lips, savouring the sticky, pungent taste of the strange moisture that covered them; the odour wafted through her flared nostrils, breathing it deep inside her body. It did strange things to her, the male odour and the pungent taste coursing through her entire being like a sweet, soothing balm, lighting tiny fires in her turgid nipples and causing a sensuous throbbing in the nerve ends of her tight, hot pussy. She could feel dew-drops of moisture rising there between her open legs as the exposed hair-lined lips began a slow spasmodic contraction, palpitating wetly.

"Ooohh, Alex, take me, darling, take me now, I need you sooo!"

Ganfeld, the little dwarf, grinned evilly, his greedy eyes feasting lewdly on her unconsciously squirming nakedness. He moved around on the bed, crouching on all fours over the white, sensuously twisting body, pushing her unresisting, milk-white thighs apart. He crawled between them, his knees pressing between her ankles and his face panting a few inches above the hair-covered triangle of her opened-wide thighs. His mouth salivated as his eyes looked down at it rotating sensuously, expectantly, just below his lips. Saliva dripped from his open mouth, mingling with her juices in the delicious, narrow split that started at the bottom of her smooth, white belly and trailed down through the rounded, creamy spheres of her buttocks.

Through half-slitted eyes Amanda could see the shadowy figure of her husband, Alex, crouching between her wide-splayed legs. She could feel the flat palms of his sweating hands pushing against the softness of her inner thighs, holding them wide apart. Her secret treasure was open to him to do as he willed. She watched with bated breath as his head lowered slowly... slowly... slowly...

And then –

"Aaahhh!" she cried, her body convulsing as his moist, hot lips closed over the soft mound at the base of her belly. His hazy face disappeared from her view into the soft pubic fleece as he planted wet, tickling kisses on the still-closed aperture, his tongue flicking lizard-like at the quivering opening.

Her own hands moved sensuously down over her throbbing breasts and slid down her smooth, flat stomach, coming to rest on either side of his lips. Her fingers stroked softly for a moment at the flexing hollows of her inner thighs, then slowly spread the fleshy, hair-rimmed lips of her moist, hot cunt apart, allowing his hungry questing lips complete access to the secret mouth down between her open thighs.

The beauteous young wife's elbows pressed tightly against her ribs and her head lolled uncontrollably from side to side on the pillow as the hot, searing tongue shot out, its soft, flicking tip circling the quivering, erected bud of her clitoris. The lips sucked, drawing the warm, soft folds deep, deep into the hot cavern of his voracious mouth, the tongue continuing its maddening licking against the straining pink button of her womanhood. She groaned deep in her throat as the hot, probing tip worked its way up and down the length of the narrow, wet slit, starting at the lower belly and pressuring its way down, down over the elastic-rimmed opening of her clasping vagina and into the crevice of her flexing buttocks where it stopped momentarily to tease the tight, brown nether-ring of the quivering anus there. Her hips ground wildly into the squeaking bed now, soft, mewling animal sounds spewing from her lips.

Ganfeld the hunchback worked hungrily, feeling the soft, wet pubic hair brushing tantalisingly against his cheeks. A feeling of power was in him. Never in his wildest dreams had he ever expected to have such a one as this squirming under his ramrod tongue and completely at his mercy. And she was loving it! Her groans drove his probe faster and faster along her moist, hot slit. He wanted her begging for it when he was ready to ram his great, oversized cock into her and she was almost there. He had never seen anyone so hot, even with the potion – and this was just the beginning!

The evil dwarf knew she was too far gone now to fight anything he did to her and his mind began to form weird erotic pictures of the positions he could put her in and the things he could do at will to her limp, desire-contorted body. He chuckled obscenely as he felt her hands desperately clawing at his hair, guiding his slickly grovelling face to the trembling opening of her cunt. He ran his tongue into the soft-fleeced flesh, flicking at it for a moment, then quickly withdrawing it to tease again around the quivering, pink edges.

Ganfeld let her force him this time, pressing his mouth directly over the tight little aperture in her squirming lower belly. As his lips rounded and covered the clasping, viscous opening, he thrust his tongue again deep down into it, bringing a low, guttural groan from the young wife whose soft, warm thighs closed convulsively around either side of his moving head. He could feel the wet flesh slip moistly around his long, extended tongue as the walls of the invaded cunt opened and closed in a hungry sucking motion, attempting to pull the probe deeper and deeper into it. He could scarcely breathe; his nose was pressed tightly against the tiny, hard clitoris, breathing in the pungent odour of her secretions and her womanhood, and it incited his penis to a hardness that he could no longer control.

He had to fuck this haughty bitch or he would explode his juices all over the mattress and her quivering, sweating flesh!

Ganfeld grabbed her flailing legs behind the knees and shoved them roughly back against her shoulders, slithering up her sweat-soaked body at the same time. His rigid cock rammed against the wet pubic hair. He planted his hands on either side of her shoulders, her ankles locked tightly behind his neck. He could look down between their bodies and see her upturned buttocks completely exposed to his lusting gaze.

The expanded, narrow cunt-slit was visibly throbbing in invitation, the wet, moist furrow held wide apart by the pressure of his thighs.

The beauteous and drugged young Amanda could see Alex hovering over her through her passion-dimmed eyes. She could feel the hugeness of his fleshy hardness lying the full length of her quivering, opened slit. The jerking head of his massive cock rested between her wide-splayed buttocks, insinuating itself up and down, up and down, in a maddening tease that caused her to twist her hips down toward it, her hungry cunt-lips searching desperately for its hard, blood-filled tip.

She had to have his great prick inside her! She had to!

The helplessly drugged young wife reached her hands down in panic beneath the grinding cheeks of her buttocks and grasped the full length of the granite-hard member. Her tightly closed fists stroked it softly, as if in reverence. She could feel the spasmodic throbbing against her soft palms and the sticky fluid that oozed in droplets from the blood-engorged head. She guided it up the valley of her vagina, not letting it lose contact with her flesh until it was poised between the moisture-covered flanges of her vagina, then placed her other hand on her husband's buttocks, drawing with all her strength to pull his cock into her screaming, quivering belly.

Ganfeld grinned obscenely above her. It was all he could do to keep from shoving forward now and impaling this squirming little bitch on his aching prick, fixing her for her scorn of him earlier, her and all her snooty goddamn kind. But he had to take it slow, slow; it was the best way. When he finally did fuck her, when he finally filled her cunt to overflowing with his boiling seed, it would be when he wanted to and not her. But the thought of that soft, warm valley around his palpitating cock caused him to involuntarily flick his hips forward, nonetheless.

Amanda felt the lips around her throbbing vagina pushed open. The elastic-rimmed tightness resisted for a moment, and then gave way before the hard, cruel pressure. The pain was harsh, for he was immense, and she mechanically resisted for a moment, emitting a long, low moan from deep within her throat.

The deformed hunchback liked that, liked to hear her cry out to him. He shoved again, harder, and was rewarded with a deeper groan. Scream, bitch! he thought wildly. Scream for mercy you'll never get from Ganfeld the hunchback!

Suddenly, then, the malformed dwarf could stand it no longer; he had to take her this moment. He rammed forward with everything he could muster, all the power in his squat, gnarled body sinking the lust-inflated cock all the way to the hilt. He could feel his balls slap tightly against her jerking anus that screwed itself down deep into the mattress in a vain attempt to escape the cruel, unexpected, brutal onslaught. Her legs jerked out wide on either side of his thick body, splaying over either edge of the bed, kicking futilely into the air.

"Uuuhhhh!" she cried with the driving pain. "Oh God, Alex, not so harrddd!

Ooohhh!"

With each forward jerk of the dwarf's body, the huge head of his great prick seemed to burrow deeper within her. His outstretched arms pinned her shoulders tightly to the mattress; his wide-spread knees held her thighs split far apart. She felt as though her body was being torn up the middle and that she would surely be ripped completely in half by this giant instrument invading her flesh. The fiery, plunging member slammed hard against her cervix, buffeting her head back harshly against the headboard of the bed.

The hunchback watched her from above with a sadistic, lascivious grin on his ugly lips. Her face was contorted with the pain of that first vicious stab. Her lips curled back from her teeth, pleading incoherently to him to be gentle, her arms flung out in a futile attempt to hold back the blunt, hard head pressing against her womb like a fiery, malevolent hand.

She'd never had it this deep before, he gloated silently. He looked down again and could see his wiry, black pubic hair tangled tightly with her soft blonde wisps, the base of his thick, fleshy rod buried deep in the pink, palpitating furrow that his tongue had licked to fire-hot receptiveness a moment ago. He could see the tight lips of the cunt stretched almost to the bursting point, the rubbery, pink outer rim clasping around his huge cock tightly.

Ganfeld held her there for a moment, savouring the spectacle of this proud little bitch impaled helplessly under him. Oh, he was going to give her a fucking she would never, never forget!

Amanda squirmed helplessly beneath the merciless cock embedded deep in her belly. She could feel the hot, searing pain of his sudden, blunt entry tearing cruelly at her insides. She flexed her hips in a vain attempt to ward off the huge invading cudgel, but the throb of her internal sinews seemed to incite it more and it ploughed its way yet deeper into her passage. She could feel every fleshy ridge of the monster alive inside her, the hard, rubbery tip pressing hard against her cervix, the thin folds of flesh along its length, the tickling hairs of his balls dangling heavily in the crevice of her soft, yielding buttocks.

And suddenly, then, in spite of her pain, young Amanda Langley began a wild licking at the wetness of her lips as paroxysms of desire flooded through her, brought about by his masterful mouth-fucking moments earlier and not destroyed by his brutal assault. Her nostrils flared again as she drew the pungent odour of his come smeared on her soft mouth once more deep into her body, mingling it in strange marriage with the feeling of the throbbing cock lodged deep in her soft, white belly. Her cunt contracted involuntarily as the lascivious spasms raced through her quivering flesh.

Ganfeld felt the slight, palpitating pressure exerted against his buried prick. He had waited for it, hovering motionless over her prostrate form patiently until she became accustomed to his thick presence rammed far up into her. He flexed gently, expanding his cock deep inside her, but still not moving his body.

"Ooohhh!" she whimpered. "Ooohhh... aaahhh!"

He waited a moment and flexed again, watching her contorted face below as another moan of rising pleasure escaped her wide-open mouth. Again he moved forward, again, again, setting a slow, teasing rhythm to his plunges. He watched her nostrils begin a slow, hesitant flaring in time to the beat of his prick, and mewling, chanting sounds of pleasure rolled unabashedly from her lips.

"Ohh, ohh, ohh, ohh, darling, darling, darling!"

Amanda's body felt itself coming to life now. The pain was receding rapidly, slowly giving way to a maddening electric tingle that began deep within her womb and seeped relentlessly through the raw nerve ends of her flesh. It rippled through her cunt and out the fleece-lined lips, dancing like fire across the milky thighs, up the full length of her wide-splayed legs, through her contracting belly and out to the tips of her pink, trembling nipples. Thin rivers of sweat rolled down the sides of the full, pulsating mounds of her heaving breasts, wetting the mattress beneath her.

She rotated her hips from side to side around the fleshy, impaling monster, her vagina dilating in time to its rhythmic hammering. It felt as though it had a heart embedded in the palpitating head whose heat against her inner passage was becoming a part of her being. She was one with it, one fleshy mass of sensation!

The evil, sadistic dwarf could hardly contain his glee as he felt her pelvis screwing up against the length of his rock-hard prick. The tiny contracting muscles inside her cunt were nibbling hungrily at the inflated head. The lips between her pink, hair-lined vaginal slit pulled tantalisingly away, sliding moistly down his rod for several inches and then nibbling slowly back up, buffering her soft blonde fur tightly against his pubic hair, embedding the full length of him deep into the warm, soft recesses. He stayed immobile, resting still above the young wife with his hands on either side of her shoulders, his knees pressed tight against the bedding. He let her quivering body pump up and down at will on his rigid, pistoning member that fused their sweating bodies together.

He could see its slow withdrawal between them, pulling thin, soft ridges of her pink flesh out with it as she screwed her pelvis down into the mattress, could see the re-entry pushing the soft folds of her pussy back into her and the moist, shiny length being swallowed whole back into her now salaciously working pussy opening. He let her strain against him for a while, watching the utter abandon of her labours, a half-mindless, ecstatic smile playing across her lips. Her motions became faster by the second, the tempo of her thrusts up against him more urgent. Ganfeld reluctantly knew she was straining to come; the juices of her milking vagina were beginning to flow and he could hear the wet sucking sound of the in-and-out sawing movement as she suddenly thrust sharply back up his cock, burying it deep inside her, her back arching a foot off the squeaking bed, her feet planted on either side of his knees tightly against the bedding. She bucked against him madly.

"Oh God, oh God, Alex darling. I'm coming, yesss, I'm coming, aahhh!"

Suddenly, with a deep-throated groan, her body began vibrating uncontrollably. Wet feminine juices oozed from her throbbing passage, drowning his impaled member with its sticky warmth and trickling down the crevice of her white, globular buttocks, inundating his hairy testicles that pressed hard against her working little anus.

The venereous hunchback went berserk as she grunted out the last of her juices against his matted pelvic region, her body still jerking spasmodically up against him. He reached back, grabbing her ankles and pushing them brutally back over her shoulders until the young wife was rolled up into a tight round ball of helplessness beneath him. Her knees were pushed back tightly over her shoulders against the mattress on either side of her flailing head, the widespread split between her legs completely open to him.

He withdrew the deeply embedded instrument of flesh until just the tip of the head rested in her. Then, he rammed forward with his stored-up, bitter dwarf's strength. She had had her fun and now it was his turn. The full palpitating length of the incited member sank cruelly into her helpless, exposed vagina. He could hear the wet, flat smacks as his belly thudded hard against her heaving crotch. His body dropped down heavily on her, mashing her full, ripe breasts tightly against his hairy, sunken chest. He locked his saliva-covered mouth over hers, thrusting his wet, dripping tongue deep into her throat, stifling the low animal grunts forming there. His shoulders pushing against the backs of her full, rounded calves kept her locked in that helpless position as he rammed his mammoth cock far up into her belly. Reaching around beneath them, he forced his hands between the mattress and the white full moons of her ass, cupping them in his spread, taloned fingers and palms, kneading the warm, soft flesh as he pulled the cheeks far apart.

Ganfeld began long, hard strokes into the steaming passage that was now wet and slippery from her climax, withdrawing the swollen head until just the tip was inside the hot, lubricious opening and then bucking forward mercilessly with his hips until his balls were screwed tightly against the wide split of her buttocks.

Young Amanda Langley groaned helplessly as her exposed cunt was plundered almost beyond endurance. He was driving her head hard back against the headboard of the bed with each jackhammer thrust and she couldn't resist from her hopelessly balled-up position. Her arms were pinned down at her sides by her own up-drawn legs. She could feel the giant glans sliding up and down inside her warm, viscous passage like a fevered piston and the hot slap of his hair-covered testicles against her trembling anus as he jerked forward on the down-stroke.

Her womb flared and the resisting lips

of her hair-fleeced furrow flowered open to receive the delicious sensations. Her hands forced themselves desperately from under her legs and snaked around his back. The long, sharp nails clawed a red streaked path over the hairy hump of his deformity, down to his flexing buttocks. She pulled him deep and thrust her fleece-covered belly up hard to skewer herself impossibly deep on the driving, hot poker of flesh. She sucked voraciously on the thick, wet tongue filling her mouth, swallowing greedily the droplets of his thick saliva. The heavy, male odour of his breath incited rather than repelled her drugged senses, and spurred her on to new heights of madness. Her body began to match his pounding lunges with her own rhythmic thrashings.

The rusty bedsprings squeaked loudly in time to the two tightly entwined bodies struggling wildly against each other. The sounds of deep, straining grunts and groans filled the hot, stifling air of the room mingling with the noise of sweat-soaked flesh smacking sharply against sweat-soaked flesh and the wet, lubricious sound of his prick sliding in and out of her warm, wet cunt.

"I'm fucking you like you've never been fucked before, fucking you like never before," the lust-crazed dwarf mumbled over and over to himself as he ceaselessly rammed the blood-filled cudgel deep into her white, screaming little belly with long cruel jabs. He could feel the hot white come building up inside his fire-hot balls as they beat hard against her upturned anus. He was ready to explode! He wildly shoved his tongue far down her throat and with harshly kneading hands pulled the widespread cheeks of her buttocks hard up against his grinding loins as he rammed his spewing cock all the way to the hilt in her soft, unresisting little cunt.

Amanda could feel her insides splitting painfully as the head of the deep-sunk, tormenting instrument suddenly flared into a hugeness that threatened to tear her apart from within. It began to spurt great, heaving torrents of fluid, and she could feel the delicious, white-hot liquid shooting into her like burning lava, ricocheting around inside her dilated stomach. The pores of her cunt clasped around it, erupting in answer and again spilling her own white-hot orgasm into the already drowning cavern of her pink, quivering channel.

She was going insane with the feel of it!

She never wanted it to end, never, never!

The totally lust-abandoned young wife reached frantically around under her squirming buttocks with both hands and began desperately to massage the balls pressed into the split of her ass. Her legs kicked out, quivering crazily in the air on either side of the bed. The huge, burrowing cock continued to jerk its completion; white-hot spurts still spewed from its head, filling her womb and foaming out of the contracting fleshy lips around the base of his great prick, soaking the soft, matted pubic hair.

"Fill me up, fill me up, Alex, darling, drown me with your cream!" she screamed incoherently around the swabbing tongue still sunk deep in her mouth. The hot walls of her spasming cunt sucked at the throbbing cock hungrily, until it gave one final spasmodic spurt, and the last drop of liquid was sucked from it by the insistent pressure.

Ganfeld, the insidious dwarf, collapsed across her body, feeling her insides still gushing forth around his deflating prick. It seemed endless, until she too suddenly gave one last thrusting jerk and quivered to a limp stillness, her legs protruding lifelessly out on either side of his fatigued body. Her arms were outstretched, one dangling doll-like over the edge of the bed. Her belly was filled to the bursting point with the dual mixture of their hot, sticky-white climaxes.

Ganfeld lay still for a moment to recover his strength and then slowly pulled himself off the comatose young wife's still form, his cock sliding slowly out of her battered pussy with a wet, slipping sound. He could see the moist, matted hair of her well-fucked young pussy glistening damply in the faint light of the room. The insides of her thighs were smeared lewdly with the white juices of their mutual passion. It dripped in tiny rivulets down the crevice of her buttocks, forming a dark wet circle on the mattress beneath her.

The malformed dwarf smiled down at her, pulling his clothes on quietly. Damn, but he'd like to fuck this hot little haughty bitch he'd so expertly enslaved a second time, but he knew he didn't have to be greedy. There would be many other times with Amanda Langley, this proud American beauty, and it would not do to glut himself with her now. Better to wait, dwelling on the next time, letting his fiery load build up again, hotter and stronger, relishing the grand fucking of her nubile young flesh so that when the moment came again, he would give it to her even more powerfully and expertly than he had only moments past.

Yes, everything was working out just fine, Ganfeld thought as he slipped out of the darkened bedroom. Amanda Langley was as good as totally debauched, even if she presently had no idea of the fact. James Figgis, his master, and Isabelle Palermo would see to the next step of the plan tomorrow.

Chapter 4

The voluptuous young blonde stirred restlessly on the rumpled guest bed. Her eyes fluttered open and fought with the darkness that permeated the thick, stale aura of the sumptuous room. Strange odours wafted through her nostrils, causing her brow to wrinkle slightly as though in deep, concentrated thought. Her tongue circled her lips, tasting the slight pungency of a sticky moistness around them.

Her eyes adjusted quizzically to the darkness and followed her form lying on the bed below. It was a strange position, she thought to herself through the haze that still dimmed her half-sleep-filled mind. Her negligee was bunched almost around her neck and she could see the twin peaks of her breasts lying loosely and her legs spread wide apart as though an invitation to some phantom lover standing at the foot of her bed.

After a moment it came to her through the dimness. The dream! The horrid, wretched nightmare which had seemed to be so real – but couldn't have been. The vividness of it began to run through her mind as though she was watching a slightly out-of-focus motion picture.

Strangely, it wasn't just her mind and soul which ached; her body was painful as well. She smoothed her hands carefully up to her breasts, cupping them gently in guarded exploration. Ohh, she moaned, they were tender. Her hands explored further, coursing their way down over her stomach to her still open thighs. She groaned again as her fingers touched tenderly the slight bruises lining the soft edges of her vagina. Her finger probed carefully around the pink, sensitive opening, the tips becoming moist from the sticky fluid that oozed viscously from it, wetting the split of her buttocks and the bed beneath.

What had happened to her? Had she done all this to herself? Had she gone to bed and dreamed first of others embracing carnality and then of a secret, shadow form tasting every part of her own being? It had seemed so real...

Isabelle and James. Rolling and panting and gasping on the living room rug in the wild frenzy of their sensual tensions. Yes, it had seemed real, but it was only an extension of her imagination; it had to be, for certainly a lady like Mrs Palermo would never allow untoward advances by a man other than her husband. Even if she was adulterous, she would not have enacted it in front of another woman! The whole situation had risen out of some dark, evil cesspool of her subconscious,

Amanda decided, and she blushed with shame at how she had mentally imagined the two friends of hers making love.

And the other, the dream of her husband visiting her and doing things to her body that she would never allow him to in actuality. She had dreamed before, had masturbated as all normal people do when frustrated sexually, but never like this! She had never gone to such an extreme even in her wildest moments of desire. Could her own hands have probed so deep into her stomach and left this hot pool that seemed to be lodged there now? Could they have made her gush forth so many times in climax to soak the bed in the way it was now? It had to be; there was no other logical explanation. She had gone completely out of her mind in her dream and had fondled her own vagina and breasts to the point of making her desires seem real. She had done these things to her own body, and her body had reacted like an animal on heat.

She slowly pushed her feet around and put them down. The fibres of the bedroom carpet felt good between her toes. She stood and looked back at the rumpled bed. Well, she thought as her eyes saw the large, round, wet spot where her buttocks had lain, I really had myself a time. I guess there's no need to cry over spilt milk; I did it and I can't change the past. After all, it was only a dream, and

I shouldn't feel ashamed over something I couldn't control.

The warm spray of the shower felt good cascading down over her body. She washed carefully the insides of her thighs and buttocks, almost reluctant to wash away the sticky, still-warm fluid from her soft pubic hair. As her fingers moved up and down the warmth of the narrow slit between her legs, cleansing it of the viscous fluid, the vision of Alex's shadowy face mashed tightly between her wide, yawning thighs seethed through her still fermenting mind. Her middle finger duplicated his lashing tongue that had flicked so maddeningly at her cunt-lips and erect bud of clitoral nerves. She leaned back against the wall and let the needles of spray beat against her breasts and raise her nipples to rock-hard excitement. She could feel her breasts harden, grow turgid with the blood of sexual heat, and her finger went a little faster, teasing her clitoris, then kneading the miniature phallus between her thumb and forefinger, and grazing the inside of her sensitive, abused vagina with her middle finger, stroking in and out, in and...

No! The pretty, blonde young woman steeled herself, stopping herself from what she thought was a repetition of what she'd done not so long ago in bed. It took all her strength to withdraw her trembling, probing fingers from down between her legs and turn off the shower.

The feeling of guilt returned as she briskly towelled herself dry with a large, fluffy Jacquard. Enough is enough! She couldn't be spending day and night playing with herself just because a couple of weird, excitingly erotic dreams had turned her on. She wasn't a nymphomaniac, for heaven's sake – but it was apparent that she needed her husband's long, stroking penis badly.

She combed out her long, silky blonde hair before the mirror, letting it drape loosely over her still taut breasts, and smiling wantonly as one sweet, pink nipple peeked coyly out of the strands in the reflection of the looking glass. "Mmm," she said to herself as she turned and opened the closet to select her clothing. She was going to be primed and ready when Alex did return all right; maybe after the way she had reacted to oral loving in her dream, she would allow him to try it on her in actuality and see if it felt as good as she thought it had last night!

She picked out a simple pair of culottes to wear, a satiny but warm covering in a colourful paisley print. She slipped on a white bra which lifted her breasts and gave them support, but kept their creamy, smooth upper portion bare; she preferred her bras like this, for they were more comfortable on her full figure. Bikini panties were all the rage, and she selected a matching white pair that barely covered her pubic mound and curly blonde hair, but she had tight buttocks that were just right for the skimpy brief. Then the culottes, and she zipped up the one-piece pantsuit with the large gold zipper which ran from her pubic triangle to neck. There was a large gold ring in the zipper fastener, which made the effect provocative. After all, she wanted to dress well after her self-inflicted orgy.

The house was quiet. Incredibly quiet, the way only a large, deserted enclosure can be. The stillness almost had a sound to it, a muffled heaviness which almost hung oppressively, mysteriously, and not at all with a sense of comfort about it. Amanda Langley slipped out of her room barefoot and padded down the long, narrow, shadowy hall toward the stairs. She recalled the fleeting and misty dream of running down this same hall last night, running blindly with horror at her heels, terror behind her and closing in fast.

How silly! Now, in the early morning hours, with only the faint rays of the violet dawn rolling across the heathered hills and seeping through the draped, arched windows, everything was normal. Quiet, but normal. She took her time, studying the large portraits on the walls, checking the little plaques nailed to the ornate gilt frames to see who the ancestors were that once lived in stately Sandaig Manor. She was dutifully impressed, as many an American is when faced with traditions dating back nearly six hundred years.

There was Archibald Figgis, a lean and gruff old man in court clothes of Edward the First, who had given the Figgises the land grant; and Montgomery Figgis, who had been thrown in prison and nearly beheaded by Cromwell, with King Charles; and Jacobsson Figgis, who sailed with Nelson and died in Egypt of some plague; the family grand-dame, Alicia Figgis, who had married into the family, outlived her husband, Gerald, and who later amassed the great fortune which still was the basis of the wealth today; the twins Jensome and Archibald Figgis, who had both joined the Hellfire Club, with which Amanda was unfamiliar, and later went to the Colonies to seek their fortunes. They were all there, proud and haughty. James Figgis, with his dark good looks and suave bearing was indeed a fine heir to the traditions and lineage of the great Figgis name.

Amanda paused beside the carved oak banister, and looked down the wide sweep of the stairs, down the wide, marble landing and the archway leading to the dining room and the broad library beyond. The young, innocent wife frowned slightly. She recalled the dinner, the tremendous, almost sybaritic feast clearly. And the lazy complacency afterwards as she sat in the library and listened to James talk politics, and the soothing effects of his modulated speech and the Grand Marnier... then what? How had she gotten to her room? Certainly not by the means she had dreamed; that was impossible to conclude in the light of day. She shook her head in confusion and some embarrassment. Perhaps she had fallen asleep or become drunk and was led upstairs, comatose.

She would ask Isabelle later, if the opportunity arose. She descended the stairs, intent on forgetting her troubled night and on seeing what the rest of the Figgis estate was like.

She wound her way through the many rooms, not hearing a sound except an occasional creaking of old wood resettling after the night coldness. She found herself eventually outside, on the wide, marble back verandah with its colonnade of stoneware and ivy, and the shallow three steps which led to an English formal garden of box hedges and grass and flower beds. She walked down and started among the hedges; the dew watered her toes and the close-cropped, spongy grass tickled the bottoms of her bare feet. She meandered, letting a contentment flow around her as the preceding events which had so upset her faded in their importance. She thought a couple of times about Isabelle and James and, yes, even the dwarf Ganfeld, but in the solitude of the garden she was happy to be alone for a while, and really wasn't concerned that they weren't up and about yet.

If she had but known where the three of them were, the young wife would surely have been horrified. In the master bedroom, which was at the end of the long second-floor hall, in the opposite wing to Amanda Langley's bedroom, the three lewd plotters lay exhausted. The night had been long, filled with rituals of pagan lust and perversion, and they were spent of energy and desire.

James Figgis lay on the round, scarlet-coverlet on the bed. He was naked, as the other two were, and he was propped up against the headboard, his legs spread wide, his penis limp and glistening against his testicles. Lying next to him was the similarly pleased Isabelle. She was on her side, propped up on one elbow, her black hair draped over the pillow, her eyes and nose level with James's genitals. Her other hand rested on his knee and her fingers toyed with his penis, trying to make him hard once more. Already the collected pools of come from many orgasms by both Ganfeld and the head of Sandaig Manor lay in her vagina... but

there was always room for more. Isabelle was a lustful, insatiable woman; she would have had it no other way.

Ganfeld was standing by the window. He had pulled the heavy crimson drapes aside partially to let in the morning sun, and he smiled as he looked out of the wavy, hand-blown glass of the small panes, out upon the formal garden beneath. He said, "It's morning. Do you want coffee or breakfast?"

"I'm full," Isabelle replied. "I'm full of you and James."

James chuckled lewdly. "I see you're still hungry, my dear. Let me rest a few minutes, and then we'll see if I can satisfy you for a little while longer."

"It's good to have you with us again, Mrs Palermo," the obsequious hunchback servant said, his gnarled back to them. "We always have so much fun together. When does your husband arrive?"

"Day after tomorrow. And he'll bring along that handsome man, Alex Langley. I hope by that time, we'll have transformed his pretty little innocent wife into a hot, raving little piece of tail."

"Have no fear. After last night..." Again Figgis chuckled. "The way she ran from us she looked as though her fanny was on fire."

"Don't laugh," Isabelle warned. "Perhaps you were wrong and she didn't get enough marijuana. Perhaps she will remember enough this morning to know it wasn't some dream but that it actually happened. Then we will lose her, her and that luscious man of hers." Her mouth trembled and a moistness formed around her lips with the sheen of anticipation. "I bet he'll be good in bed; I can't wait to find out."

The ugly, toad-like dwarf turned his head slightly and leered over his deformed shoulder at the luscious woman sprawled on the rumpled round bed. "She was completely out of it, Mrs Palermo. If the marijuana she smoked wasn't enough, I can assure you that the potion in her sherry did the trick."

"It had to be for you to fuck her first," James exclaimed. "And kiss her cunt and put your overgrown cock into her mouth. Goddamn, I wish I'd been there to watch!"

"Watch? Hell, you'd have joined right in, you sadistic beast." The glitter in Isabelle's eyes told all; she, too, would have been party to the acts that had been performed on the naïve Mrs Langley. Would have been – and was planning to just as soon as possible.

"What is the next move in our plan, master?" Ganfeld asked, turning back to the window, moving the drapes a little more so he could view the expanse of hills and the gardens. "We have to move fast if we are to have her at our mercy in two days."

"Anxious to have another go at her, aren't you, my little fiend?" James chortled and shifted his body so that his hardening prick could be better attended to by the teasing hand of the black-haired harlot beside him. "Ahh, that's it, Isabelle. More, more. Suck it, if you like." Isabelle Palermo dipped her head and slipped her lips over his turgid penis, licking his great shaft and its head with her tongue. James said, "To answer you, Ganfeld, it depends on how Mrs Langley reacts to everything that happened to her. She's a sexy little girl, she is, so I think her reaction will be…"

"She's outside," the dwarf interrupted in an excited voice. "She's wandering through the back and… and she's heading for the hut!"

"We must stop her!" Isabelle said, jerking upright.

"No, let her see the little surprise in the hut." James Figgis's eyes filmed over with the image of the lusting perversions which awaited the blonde wife. "It won't be long before she'll be formally introduced." He laughed loudly to himself. "Until she becomes old and close friends."

"She's almost there…" Ganfeld clutched the curtains with excitement.

"Isabelle, get dressed and go downstairs," James instructed.

"To stop her?"

"No, I said that I want her to go in. If she's near the hut and doesn't decide to see what's inside, then get her to. And if she does on her own, then I want you to be ready to comfort her. She'll need comforting after the shock she's going to get, and you're just the one for that."

"And then?" Isabelle was breathless with anticipation of what was to come. "And... and then what?"

"Bring her to the living room." The evil Lord of Sandaig Manor grinned sardonically, his face lined with the effects of his debauchery. "No; better yet, bring her to my study. Ganfeld, prepare more of the sherry. We want to be ready when the poor young Mrs Langley begins to comprehend what is happening."

And with that, Figgis once again began to laugh diabolically, and he was joined by the throaty purring of Isabelle Palermo and the high, hysterical tittering of the gnarled dwarf.

* * *

Amanda Langley turned to look back in the direction from which she had come. The high green hedges were like a natural barricade between her and the mansion; she could see the monster house of stone loom over her, but the long porch and most of the first floor were hidden from view. She thought she saw the curtains in a window on the second floor move, as if rustling in the morning breeze. But there wasn't any wind; nothing stirred except perhaps the curtain. From somewhere out on the endless hills came soft, distant calling of sheep, and once there was the bark of a dog, then nothing. She turned around and continued her way through the winding paths, pleasantly pleased by the well-tended, circular beds of flowers, at the stone benches held up by stone lions and gargoyles...

The main path, bordered by thin, almost wispy trees, seemed to lead in a roundabout fashion to the left-hand corner of the garden. Up ahead she could see the old mortised brick wall that was mostly covered with ivy that bordered the garden, setting it apart from the purple and black table that was the moor. She turned the last corner and spied a tall round building made of stone.

It was one of the oddest small buildings Mrs Langley had ever seen. It looked older than the ancient house, its stonework rough-hewn and crumbling at the corners, as if the prehistoric Druids had fashioned it crudely as some enclosed place of dark worship. Ivy, the broad-leaved British variety, and moss grew on it, but unlike the healthy and bright, deep greenness of the plants among the garden wall, the gnarled and twisted branches of the growth on the building were blighted and a sick brown, and the leaves seemed to curl inward and wilt, and the moss was sparse and burnt-looking. Moreover, while the garden wall was covered from top to bottom, the lushness spilling over its top like zealous escapees, the ivy and moss finally gave up after no more than six feet in height along the building's surface, as though there was something in the stone which prevented and stunted what lay upon it.

The small house was circular, like a cistern or guardhouse, or a turret of some medieval castle, with a tall, peaked roof made of some undefinable thatch or thin shingle. The only windows were small slits, the type which widened out on the inside on an angle so that archers and other defenders could operate behind cover, and what little area was exposed was barred with thick iron scrollwork. The wrought iron had once been blackened; now it was rusty and pitted, and where it was fastened to the wall by great bolts, the stone was stained with orange-yellow streaks.

The building made Amanda Langley falter for a minute and hold her breath, for somehow its very existence ruined the placid morning, causing a great chill to travel her spine and dig at the pit of her stomach. Yet there was a fascination to it; a spellbinding intrigue about why it was there, what it was for – the secrets of its interior. She hesitated, and put one dainty foot forward as though testing the path that led around it, as though the round stone house might have a way of stopping an intruder from interrupting its gloomy loneliness.

Then she smiled. This was no way to be, she chastised herself. After all, there is nothing there to harm me, no hidden mystery that could make trouble if I came closer. Get hold of yourself, you silly goose! Your imagination is running rampant, just as it did last night... and you know what that caused!

Her morale boosted by her pep talk, Amanda continued. She came right up to the building and felt the cold, clammy exterior, and laughed as indeed, nothing did happen to her, that she wasn't struck down. She walked along the path; it curved around and the grass faded away as the ivy had, and flinty gravel made her feet hurt. She considered whether she should go back.

And then she saw the door. It was set well in an arch of capped stone, shadows making it look heavier and blacker than it actually was. It was of old, hewn oak, sections the size of house beams welded together by bands and studs of thick metal, and hinges monstrous in size cemented to the wall and attached to the door with long, spear-like extensions. There was a large ring for the handle, and below it a keyhole that looked as if it was part of a lock rugged enough to withstand the most ardent assault. Hanging on a peg set in the stone was a key, an old-fashioned one with a long shank and a big, ornate head.

Should she? Her heart hammered at her breast, and there seemed to be a constriction in her lungs. A quick peek... the curiosity was almost too much for Amanda to bear! Who would know if she took down the key, fitted it in the antique lock and opened the door?

She turned away. No, that would be prying. Anyway, it was probably no more than a garden shed for the tools and equipment used in tending the garden. That's all there was inside... or was it? She stopped and looked back at the door. It seemed to beckon her, to invite her to investigate the dark depths of its insides. And yet the rest of the building let off the distinct impression of alienness, of rejection. The tall, blonde woman shuddered at the deliciously enervating ambivalence of her feelings. It was all in her mind, of course...

She started back toward the mansion. She'd ask James what the stone hut was used for, and perhaps he would take her to it. But she knew that wouldn't really be the way of resolving the romantic involvement she had started with the house; no, she would have to conquer her own curiosity and imagination and go back and see. Nobody was around, nobody would know, and the whole idea of it was like something she had read as a little girl, like *The Secret Garden*, or *The Wizard of Oz*. She wasn't so old as to have lost all of her kittenish ways.

She ran to the hut, her mind resolved to do the forbidden. Down came the key! She fit the key into the mortise lock and jiggled it around, waiting for the latch to trip. There was a loud click and she leaned against the ring and shoved against the door. The door protested with a loud squeal of hinges.

The interior was dark. It was also dank and smelled oddly of old straw and dry rot, but the floor was of packed earth and there wasn't any wood to be seen other than the door. She licked her lips nervously and opened the door wider. The morning sun fell across the floor in a wide shaft, highlighting the empty, barren area in front of the door. A spider scurried across the wall, frightened by the sudden light. Amanda stepped inside and peeked; the gloom was thick and cloying like a grey muslin sheet and she could not see farther than the light no matter how hard she squinted. She let the door swing wide then, letting as much light as she could invade the inky, dungeon atmosphere.

Then she saw a plain, plank table. On

it were a stack of magazines and a large enamelled bowl that was curiously filled with fruit. She could see a couple of apples, some oranges, and if her eyes weren't deceiving her, a bunch of bananas behind it. Frowning, her curiosity peaked to its fullest, Amanda stepped to the table. What on earth would a bowl of fruit and magazines be doing in a place like this? She picked up one of the magazines. The magazines were digest-sized, with plain brown covers. She held some up to the light. Written on each cover was the title, *Climax Illustrated*, and then different volume numbers. She thumbed through volume seven, at first only mildly interested, and then in sudden revulsion she dropped the little booklet and put her hands across her mouth in disbelief.

The booklet fell open on the table. What she saw was now before her in twice the blazing colours – a two-page spread in full clear tones and exact detail of three men and two women together on an immense double bed. The five persons were naked and what they were doing to one another sent ripples of further revulsion travelling up her back. The man on the extreme left was lying with his huge penis in the foreground at full erection. Straddling it with an expression of pure ecstasy was a large, well-built Negro woman, her vagina and breasts in full display, a black satin goddess enjoying lusty human pursuits. Besides the couple was another, with the girl on all fours like an animal. She was blonde and fair, and looked more than a little like Amanda, although more Scandinavian in features. Standing at the side of the bed was a Negro man, his muscles etched across his body, and his black, curly pubic hair nearly impossible to see against his burnished, prune-coloured body. His cock made a wonderful contrast of colour as it penetrated the golden fleece of the girl's upturned pubic area, slid between her spread buttock cheeks and nestled home in her pink-rimmed vagina. And as if that wasn't enough to glaze the eyes of the distraught young wife who looked at them, there was a third man who was kneeling in front of the white woman. His tremendous cock, in horizontal rigidity, was at the lips and mouth of the girl, its bulbous red glans, so glaringly in focus, resting on the outstretched tongue of the girl. Her lips were pulled back as if supplicating for its full length to be slid into her hungry mouth.

And then, before even the wretchedness of what she was viewing settled in her shattered mind, Amanda heard something rustle behind her! For one terrified moment she stiffened; it was as if her whole body was of chipped ice, an immobile statue. Then there was a louder scraping sound, a heavy, regulated breathing. She whirled round and screamed.

There, dimly visible in the light, loomed a monster! A thick animal, a stout beast, terribly hairy. It wasn't as tall as she was, and it was hunched over, its muscular arms dragging on the dirt, its knuckles making noises.

An ape!

Amanda stumbled backwards, every fibre in her body in turmoil as the ugly creature studied her with small, very dark eyes. Its rubbery lips parted and it sniffed the air, making the same snuffing sound as she had heard before, and then it stood erect. It grunted and panted and tried to close the gap between them, its desire more pronounced than ever. But it couldn't... around its right leg was a tight metal band, and to the band was a thick chain which led into the invisible recesses of the building. For one instant Amanda dared to breathe, for she saw the chain and clamp, and knew that the ape couldn't touch her. She backed against the table, her whole being still in shock, unable to comprehend what to do.

The ape yanked at the chain, its great leathery paws digging at the ground in a vain attempt to free itself, and it seemed to whine with frustration. With the first impact of horror past, Amanda Langley also became aware that the ape was not angry or belligerent, but was acting as if it wanted to be friendly. It seemed as if it was looking for affection the way a dog might. She hesitated.

And then she let her vision wander down the thick, shaggy stomach and to the huge, dangling, hair-covered shaft of the ape's penis. A male... a fantastically huge male with a penis that seemed to be totally out of proportion to its size, Amanda blushed, though her eyes kept staring at his groin, and then as if in response, the ape's cock began to swell and perk upwards until it no longer hung downward like a third small arm but instead reared upwards in a decided curve.

The ape was excited. It was ready for intercourse... with her! Amanda let out another stifled scream, more of outraged revulsion than terror, and turned and fled from the round little building. She stumbled down the garden path, tears once more stinging her eyes at the thought of what was in the animal mind of the ape. She flung her head back and forth and staggered in blind hysteria.

And almost threw Isabelle Palermo down on the ground in her haste to get away. Isabelle steadied the sobbing wife, putting her arms around her in a show of feminine concern, and even patted her back. Isabelle knew exactly what kind of experience Amanda had had seconds earlier, though she acted otherwise.

"A... an ape! There's an ape in that... that house back there!" Amanda was uncontrollable and choking on her words.

"For heaven's sake, calm down, Amanda," Isabelle said in soothing tones as she lied to still the younger woman's fears. "Of course there is. That's only Genghis, though, and he's not really an ape. Only a very harmless, very tame chimp."

"But... but he's so big!" In her mind came the vision of the monster penis, but Amanda couldn't tell her friend that she was thinking of his male member when she said he was so big.

"Chimps normally are around five feet tall, Amanda, and weigh about 130 or so pounds. They're very intelligent, you know, and highly sociable."

"What... what's it doing here?"

"I'll tell you on the way back to the house. James is in the study, I believe. He sent me out to look for you." They started along the path, Isabelle giving the still distraught young wife support. "James's father, Christopher Figgis, brought Genghis home from tropical Africa as a baby chimp. Been part of the family for all these years; James played with Genghis as a child. Normally James lets the chimpanzee have complete freedom of the garden, and that's why there are such high walls around it. But he thought it best with you coming that he chain the beast up."

"Oh... Oh, I see," sobbed Amanda.

"Anybody would have been frightened at first. You should have been told. Come on, Amanda. We'll go to see James and have a nice comforting glass of sherry to calm your nerves. Won't that be nice?"

Chapter 5

James Figgis was standing before the fireplace when the two women entered the library, and he studied the young blonde wife carefully as Isabelle led her across to the wide leather couch near the roaring blaze. Ah, good, good, he thought, barely able to conceal his elation. She's seen Genghis, and judging from the whiteness of her face she perused my little collection of Copenhagen art, too! Things are progressing quite nicely, and it will only be a matter of moments now before I can possess that fine, voluptuous young body, those soft, warm red lips...

Expertly concealing his inner gloating, for he had had long practice at such veilings, the wealthy Lord of Sandaig Manor put on a grave, concerned expression as he approached the two women. "Why, Amanda, my dear, what's the matter? You're as pale as a ghost. Did something frighten you?"

"I... I accidentally found your... pet," murmured Amanda as Isabelle sat her down on the couch. "He... frightened me for just a moment..."

"Ah, yes, Genghis," said James smoothly. "But how stupid of me to have neglected to tell you about him; I should have expected that you would be exploring the garden. Can you forgive me such an oversight, my dear?"

"Why... yes, of course, James." Amanda favoured him with a meagre smile, while Isabelle patted her hand reassuringly.

"Let me get you a glass of sherry," said James solicitously. "It will make you feel much better."

"Yes, I think I'd like some sherry."

James smiled, his eyes touching Isabelle's briefly. Then he went to the handsome bar and poured a large glass full of ruby liquid from a decanter which sat atop the counter – a decanter which Ganfeld had gleefully placed there only minutes earlier. He carried the glass back to the couch, sitting down on the other side of Amanda from Isabelle, and handed the blonde wife the sherry.

Amanda accepted the glass gratefully and raised it to her lips. She was still upset – she could not help but think about those awful, terrible booklets she had seen in the ape's stone hut, and wonder why they were there, whose they were; she wanted to ask James about them, but she couldn't seem to bring herself to voice the words. She had experienced the same difficulty even with Isabelle, her best friend, in the garden moments ago.

The beauteous American girl drank deeply of the warm, syrupy liquid, feeling it coursing the length of her throat and settling with a pleasant glow in her stomach. She did not see, as she drained the glass, the shining eyes of James Figgis and Isabelle Palermo, the lascivious eagerness in their momentarily unguarded faces.

Amanda placed the empty glass on one of the nearby tables, then leaned back, closing her eyes. I wish I'd never consented to come here, she thought. First that awful dream last night, and then waking up to find I'd lost control of myself in my sleep and orgasmed, and then seeing the ugly chimpanzee with its monstrous penis and those evil, filthy pornographic booklets... This isn't turning out to be a quiet, relaxing vacation at all; it's turning into a... a kind of nightmare, in which everything seems pleasant and nice on the surface, but underneath all is evil and perverted. I'm going to ask Alex to take me back to London, to take me home, as soon as he returns from Genoa.

Amanda let her thoughts trail off as a strange sort of dreamy torpor seemed to envelop her whole being. She lay relaxed against the couch, between Isabelle and the Lord of Sandaig Manor, and suddenly she felt at ease, felt as if she were safe and protected. She seemed to realise, deep down, that this wasn't true – but the feeling persisted in her conscious mind. Her head was feathery-light, and her stomach and loins seemed to glow with pleasant warmth. Odd... her nipples were hardening beneath the pantsuit she wore, and... and she could feel a tingling of sexual desire in the soft, moist folds of her pussy...

Time seemed to stand still for Amanda Langley, and it was as if she began drifting on a soft, fleecy cloud of torpor. Yes, and it was as if hands, so soft and gentle, were beginning to caress her flesh slowly, tantalisingly, expertly moving over her breasts and her belly and her warmly flowering cunt, exciting her, soothing her, such nice, nice feelings...

If the young wife had known that her dreamy thoughts were more than merely mental – that soft, gentle hands were indeed moving slowly, soothingly, over her still body at that moment – she would have been shocked and horrified. But she did not know, had no awareness that both James Figgis and her best friend, Isabelle Palermo, were caressing her with their talented fingers; she did not know that what was causing her to feel so dreamy and floating was the potion, the powerful and carefully dosed aphrodisiac made by the evil dwarf, Ganfeld; she did not know that the gentle caresses, part of the plan mapped out by James and Isabelle to put young Amanda at her ease in the beginning, would soon become something entirely different, something brutal and lusting and depraved.

His long-fingered hands deftly fondling the firm, resilient tits of the American girl, tweaking the nipples into heated arousal, the Lord of Sandaig Manor nodded his head to Isabelle Palermo, grinning obscenely as he did so. The black-haired Englishwoman, whose own grin matched James's in lewdness, removed her own fingers from the slightly protuberant mound of Amanda Langley's womanhood, where they had been kneading and stroking the soft, warm cunt into secreting excitation; she reached down to the table and lifted the lid on the silver cigarette box there, removing one of the crude brown cylinders which Amanda had so innocently smoked the night before. Then Isabelle placed the marijuana cigarette between the blonde young wife's red lips as Figgis continued to caress her, and Amanda offered no objection.

Isabelle struck a match, lighting the joint, and then she whispered softly, mesmerically, "Inhale deeply, dear Amanda. Inhale... inhale... deeply... deeply... yes, that's it, dear... that's very nice. You feel so good, don't you? You feel so very good..."

"Yes, oh yes," the beauteous blonde girl replied, and she did feel good... peaceful and warm and safe and... yes, sexually stimulated, too. Was Alex there? Oh, she hoped he was, she wanted him very much just now... wanted his hard, masculine penis moving deep inside her, bringing about their simultaneous orgasm as it always did... his lovely, warm, hard cock deep, deep, deep inside her...

"Alex... Alex!" she whimpered, beginning to undulate her lithe, sculpted body under the manipulations of Figgis and Isabelle. The dark-haired woman held the cigarette butt between Amanda's lips, whispering, telling her that everything was all right, everything was fine... inhale... inhale... deeply... deeply...

Amanda settled back again, lulled into drowsy security by the comforting, seemingly far away sound of her friend's voice, obeying the order to inhale the warm, sweetish smoke which filled her lungs again and again. But the stimulation had not dissipated at all, for her pussy was tingling deliciously, her nipples were very hard, and she still had the sensation of being tenderly, relentlessly caressed.

Isabelle Palermo looked across at the Lord of Sandaig Manor, mouthing a question with her lips. "Is she ready, do you think?"

James nodded. Isabelle removed her hands from the young girl's body, leaning close to her ear and breathing very softly against her soft, warm neck. Figgis's fingers continued to lightly stroke Amanda's firmness through the culottes she wore.

"Amanda," Isabelle whispered, "Amanda, can you hear me, dear?"

"Yes," came the immediate answer. "Yes, Isabelle, I can hear you."

"It's terribly warm in here, isn't it?"

"Warm?"

"Yes... you're very warm, aren't you? It's very hot in this room, Amanda. Wouldn't it be nice to take those culottes off that you're wearing?"

"No... yes... Isabelle, I..."

"Shhh, dear, you're with Isabelle, aren't you? You're with your friend..."

"Yes... yes..."

"Wouldn't you like to take off your culottes, Amanda dear? Wouldn't you like to be comfortable instead of so warm and hot? Wouldn't you like to feel the glow of the fire on your bare, naked skin? Wouldn't you, Amanda, wouldn't you?"

The beauteous blonde wife squirmed

restlessly on the couch, her eyes squeezed tightly shut and her face drawn into a frown. The combined drugs of marijuana and Ganfeld's insidious aphrodisiac potion, the power of Isabelle's soft, suggestive, hypnotic voice, had brought beads of sweat popping out on Amanda's smooth forehead. She was hot... she was almost suffocating in her culottes. She wanted to take them off – Isabelle was right – but... but not here... James, James was here... she couldn't...

"You want to make yourself naked, don't you, Amanda?" droned the black-haired woman's voice. "You want to be completely naked and comfortable, I know you do."

"Yes... yes... but I... I..."

"Are you worried about James?" asked Isabelle. "You needn't, dear, not at all. James has gone up to his room. He won't be back down for a long time."

"He... he won't...?"

"No, of course he won't. You don't have to worry, now do you, Amanda dear? You can make yourself naked in complete comfort, without any fears at all. I'm going to take my clothes off, dear. You see, I'm warm and hot too. I want to be naked, just like you do."

"You... do?"

"Yes, of course I do," Isabelle intoned. "I'm undressing right now. I'm taking my clothes off right here and now, Amanda, just as you're going to do in a moment..."

As she spoke, the confidently smiling Englishwoman began to shed her heavy winter dress. She wore only a pair of brief panties beneath it, and she was soon free of those. She stood in her naked splendour, her black pubic triangled pussy already beginning to seep the juices of her growing excitement at what was about to happen to the young girl next to her. Her small, well-rounded breasts were sheened with sweat, and the nipples quivered pinkish-brown and rigid on their crests. She smiled lewdly at James, as his eyes travelled wantonly over the symmetrical loveliness of her mature body; he never ceased to become aroused by this wicked, amoral bitch with the insatiable mouth and cunt...

Still smiling, Isabelle quickly sat back down and took Amanda Langley's hand in her own. She began crooning to her again, "I'm naked now, Amanda dear, and it's lovely... so lovely. The fire feels so nice on my bare skin and I'm not hot any more... oh, it really is wonderful, my pet..."

"Isabelle... Isabelle, are you really naked...?"

"Of course I am, Amanda. Here, give me your hand." The dark-haired Palermo woman took the young American girl's hand and guided it slowly over the bare flesh of her thigh, upward over the satiny smoothness of the flat stomach, and then held it tightly to one perfectly rounded tit for a long moment before releasing it. Her cunt churned with excitement at the electric contact of the other woman's fingers, and she knew she was building to another of her magnificent climaxes. Oh God, this was going to be a satisfying experience! Never had she wanted to completely debauch a young, tender innocent like she wanted to subjugate and convert Amanda Langley!

"Do you see, my sweet?" she droned on. "I'm naked... completely naked... just as you should be naked..."

"Yes..." moaned Amanda, completely under the power of the older woman's hypnotic voice, and the drugs working in her body and brain. "Yes... I want to be naked, Isabelle... help me get naked, Isabelle, my friend..."

James Figgis's mouth salivated at the prospect of soon fucking this desirable young American – and at the salacious sight of Isabelle Palermo's nakedness so provocatively displayed before his lusting eyes. His prick was already hard in his pants, screaming for release from its encumbering clothing, and he knew he would obey the urgent plea of his manhood in just a few more minutes. But first...

He helped Isabelle raise the loose, unresisting form of Amanda Langley into a sitting position and then held her there while the dark-haired woman deftly hooked her finger through the zipper ring on the front of the pantsuit and drew it down from throat to abdomen. James's breath quickened as he saw the glistening naked flesh of Amanda's stomach, the way her breasts spilled over the uplifting half-bra, the flimsy panties encasing the soft, pulsating mound of her womanhood.

Isabelle slid to the floor, grasping the bottoms of the culottes and drawing them hurriedly down and off, so that Amanda now sat in nothing but the thin, filmy undergarments. With quick expertise, the evil older woman unfastened the bra straps, pulling the garment away and allowing the rich, firm, milky-white splendour of the American girl's breasts to be exposed to the lewd gaze of the Lord of Sandaig Manor, the exquisite nipples and areolae distended and seeming to pulse as if with a life of their own atop the snowy hills. Then Isabelle's fingers dipped down to the band of Amanda's briefs, and as James gently guided the young girl's hips up off the couch, Isabelle drew the panties down and tossed them with the discarded culottes. Amanda Langley, like Isabelle, was at last naked, completely defenceless with all her charms exposed before the hungrily devouring eyes of the two older people.

"How does it feel to be naked, Amanda

dear?" Isabelle crooned into the young wife's ear. "Isn't it lovely to be without those hot clothes? Isn't it nice to be as nude as I am?"

"Oh yes!" agreed Amanda, mesmerised. She squirmed her body luxuriously on the cool leather of the couch. Oh, it really was nice, her drugged mind thought. So lovely and nice... especially without those constricting bra and panties... her breasts felt so good and tingly, free, with the warmth of the fire trailing over them, bringing the nipples into almost painful hardness... and down between her legs, a throbbing ecstasy, an arousal she had not felt in a long time... her brain was spinning warmly, giddyingly, and she felt as if she were drunk, drunk on desire and passion... Alex, oh Alex, I wish you were here right now...

Isabelle intoned, "You're comfortable, aren't you, Amanda? Nice and naked and not too hot and very comfortable, aren't you?"

"Yes, oh yes!"

"Fine," Isabelle drawled insidiously, "that's fine, dear. Now then, tell Isabelle what you saw when you entered the stone hut in the garden a little while ago."

A small frown furrowed the young wife's forehead, as if the question didn't quite penetrate the fog of her spinning mind. Then she gave her head a tiny little shake, seeming to comprehend at last the sudden change in conversational direction, and said, "What... what I saw?"

"Yes. What did you see, dear? Tell me what you saw."

"The... the ape..." mumbled the young blonde girl.

"Yes – Genghis. But what else did you see, Amanda? Wasn't there something else you saw in the hut?"

"No... no..."

"Of course there was," went on Isabelle soporifically, relentlessly. "You remember, dear Amanda. There were some booklets, weren't there? Some booklets on the table..."

"Booklets," Amanda repeated, and her marijuana- and aphrodisiac-drugged mind repeated the word over and over again. She couldn't talk about those filthy, lewd things... she couldn't... and yet Isabelle was her friend and she felt so wonderful without her clothes, safe and warm and nice... and she was so naughtily excited, her pussy flowering her juices of passion forth – and the image of the photographs in the booklets, enticing and boldly obscene, made her vagina tingle even more with forbidden ardour.

"Tell me what you saw in the booklet, Amanda," Isabelle whispered in her ear. "You did see them, didn't you? You did look at them, didn't you?"

"Yes... yes... they were filthy...

pornography..."

"What did they depict, Amanda?"

"Men... men and women... five of them... together..."

"What were they doing?"

"Ohhh... awful things, terrible things..."

"What kind of things?"

"No! I... I can't tell you..."

"Of course you can, dear," Isabelle said, enjoying herself immensely now. James had told her about leaving the copies of *Climax Illustrated* in Genghis's hut, so that the innocent young woman would hopefully stumble on them – and she had, just as James had said she might. She continued, "Just relax, dear, and tell Isabelle exactly what the people in the booklets were doing."

"They... they were... oh God, they were making love and... and..."

"Yes? And what, Amanda? And what?"

"And kissing... kissing one another between the legs!" wailed the beauteous blonde wife piteously. "There... there was this blonde girl and she... she... she had this huge Negro's... penis between her lips."

"She was sucking him, wasn't she?" Isabelle crooned. "She was sucking the Negro's cock, wasn't she, Amanda?"

"Isabelle!"

"Oh, it's all right, dear, it's all right. It's just woman talk between us, you know.

That's what she was doing, wasn't it? She was sucking him off, wasn't she?"

"Y-yes... yesss..."

Isabelle, her lips curled in a lascivious grin of delight, slid off the couch then and dropped onto her knees on the carpet before the fireplace. Only seconds before, the Lord of Sandaig Manor, now divest of his own clothes, had stretched out supine, his giant rock-hard cock jutting upward like a huge spear from his trembling loins. His legs were spread wide and Isabelle crawled between them, kneeling with her head lowering almost to the tip of his great cock. She took the fleshy, palpitating instrument between her hands and began to rub it lightly with the palms, arousing the evil master of the baronial mansion to a fever pitch; it was all he could do to keep from moaning and writhing under her expert ministrations – but it wasn't time yet, not just yet... this had to be done just right in order to keep the young blonde American wife in her mesmerised state.

Isabelle turned her head and spoke up to Amanda, who was sitting in a dazed stupor with her legs slightly spread on the couch, the curling blonde hairs fringing her warm, wet pussy so provocatively presented to the feasting eyes of the lusting couple on the floor. The young wife's thighs rippled with desire, and her breasts rose and fell with her ragged breathing. Her eyes were still squeezed tightly shut, and her hands were clenched into fists at her sides.

"The girl in the booklet was sucking a man's penis, Amanda," Isabelle whispered. "Sucking it hard and enjoying it, wasn't she?"

"Oohhhh," moaned the drugged, desire-ridden girl on the couch. "Yes, yes, yes!"

"Have you ever done that to Alex, Amanda? Have you ever sucked him with your mouth?"

"Isabelle, don't... don't talk like that!"

"Have you, Amanda? Have you, my sweet?"

"I... I..."

"Tell me, now. Tell Isabelle, your friend."

"I-I've only kissed the t-tip... only once or twice. It's... it's wrong..."

"No, it's wonderful. It's the most wonderful thing in the world, my dear girl."

"No... no..."

"Oh yes, it's wonderful. I've been sucking cock for a long, long time now and it's wonderful, marvellous. I've been sucking Sebastian's cock and I've been sucking James's too. I like the taste of James's cock, Amanda. It tastes so good... so good... so good..."

"No!" came the anguished wail of despair

from Amanda Langley. What was she hearing? Was this Isabelle, her friend, speaking to her this way? No... no... she was having another one of those awful, terrible nightmares like last night... yes that was it, a nightmare, a sex nightmare, because her vagina ached with desire and her passion flowed hotly along her thighs, causing her to open and close them spasmodically.

"Yes, Amanda, oh yes. I'm going to suck James now, right here in this room, and you're going to watch me do it. You're going to watch, and then, after a while, you're going to take my place, Amanda. You're going to suck James's cock, you're going to take it between those soft red lips of yours and suck him and suck him and suck him until he comes hot and sticky into your mouth and you swallow it into your belly..."

"No! Oh dear God above, no, no, NO!"

"Yes, Amanda, yes, you're becoming so excited now that you can't stand it... you're burning up with sexual fever and the sight of my mouth around James's cock will almost drive you mad with desire and lust... you're going to watch, Amanda, watch and then take my place... watch and take my place... watch and take my place..." On and on the evil black-haired woman's voice droned, burning its way through every cell of the young blonde girl's brain.

Amanda's mind tried to reject the awful

words, the terrible perverted commands – but it was powerless under the combined forces of the marijuana and the aphrodisiac potion and the hypnotic power of Isabelle Palermo's words. It's a dream, she thought desperately, a nightmare, it has to be a nightmare... this can't be really happening, oh God help me, this can't really be happening!"

"When I count to three," Isabelle purred, "you're going to open your eyes and watch. You're not going to be able to move, only sit there and watch and become more and more excited. You're going to become so hot you'll feel like you're on fire, and then you'll cry out to me that it's your turn and you'll take my place. Do you understand, Amanda?"

No, no, no! a small rational corner of her brain screamed in agonised protest. But it was powerless against the evil forces dominant there. Amanda Langley said, "Yes... y-y-yes, I... I understand..." in a voice that was so strange and thick she did not even recognise it as her own.

"Good, good," cooed Isabelle Palermo, and then she slowly, with tongue-moistened lips glistening, lowered her head forward and down, her incredibly hot, soft mouth closing over the sensitive head of James Figgis's lustfully throbbing cock.

The young blonde wife's eyes fluttered open, blinked several times, and then focused clearly. The horror of the sight which assailed them – a sight of her best friend, Isabelle, with her lips closed around the huge, up-thrust penis of the Lord of Sandaig Manor – sent violent tremors of revulsion coursing through her body. The small corner of her brain screamed for her to run, to get out of there, because this was not a nightmare – and neither had last night been a nightmare! This was real! But her body didn't obey. The hot passion in her loins was enough to keep her rooted where she was, aware and yet not caring about her total nakedness, the full splendour of her softly hair-fringed cunt-lips opened wide, secreting her passion down the inside of her thighs.

She could only sit there and stare out of protuberant eyes at the salaciously naked couple on the floor before her. The realisation of what was really going on at Sandaig Manor was dimly present in her drugged brain, but somehow that didn't seem to matter either. She was too excited, too much under the strange hypnotic spell cast upon her by Isabelle Palermo, to care about anything but the sight of James Figgis's huge, blue-veined penis sliding hotly, wetly between the convoluting lips of the black-haired woman kneeling on all fours between his wide-splayed thighs.

Isabelle's firebrand tongue licked circles of liquid fire around and around the sensitive, quivering head of Figgis's pulsating cock, flicking into the glans opening, drinking up the lubricating fluid flowing there. His hands reached up involuntarily and tangled in her short-clipped hair, trying to guide her head further down to meet his violent upward thrusts into her face, driving the length of his massive member deep into the soft, warm folds of her mouth, slamming it up hard against the back of her throat.

"Uuummm!" mewled Isabelle around the hardened rod of flesh.

"Aaahhh!" James cried in lust-crazed agreement.

Isabelle drew back slightly so that she was able to taste the moist stickiness of the glans again, twirling her tongue maddeningly faster around the blood-inflated head. Then she began to suck him rhythmically, with all the practised expertise of the accomplished female harlot. Figgis watched her convoluted lips working on his cock and tried to think that it would be the lips of Amanda Langley very soon now... but Isabelle was too good, too expert to allow him to think about anything except the delicious sensations of pure delight which coursed through his quivering shaft from her tantalisingly expert ministrations. Through glazed eyes he saw the soft, wet skin of her mouth pucker outward and then back in again as she raised and lowered her mouth the full length of his rigid member, and his loins tensed and jerked upward into her face, all the fleshy expanse disappearing with each hard forward thrust, so that only a small stretch of it showed white and glistening with saliva wetness between her glistening red lips.

Her tongue, with a nerve-shattering lick on the outstroke, was like a separate entity, a thing gone wild with sheer animal lust, making the quivering, palpitating head jerk and convulse crazily as though it, too, were a thing alive with a desire of its own. She sucked hungrily, her mind caught up in the task of what she was doing but not as fully concentrating on extracting his fiery-hot semen from his balls as it would have been under different circumstances. Even as she sucked, her breasts dancing below her torso, her free hand tickling and caressing the sperm-bloated sac of James Figgis's churning testicles, her ears were attuned to catch the slightest sound from the drug- and hypnosis-enslaved young girl on the couch – a young girl who was about to be totally and irrevocably broken, subjugated, as so many had been at Sandaig Manor in the past.

On the couch, Amanda Langley gazed with intoxicated rapture at the lascivious sight before her on the floor, made devilish and eerie by the flickering glow of the fire in the inglenook. Her mouth hung slack in ecstatic captivation, and her eyes were glassy and lust-smoked. She watched thin rivulets of saliva trickle out of the corners of her girlfriend's mouth as she voraciously sucked James Figgis's penis, and empathetic ribbons of her own saliva made her lips and mouth and chin glisten in the light.

Look at the way she draws his huge rod into her mouth, as if it were a delicious peppermint candy cane, thought the piteous young blonde wife, mesmerised. It's terrible and wicked and evil, oh God, I should be sick watching such a lewd thing... but I'm so excited I can hardly stand it. I'm on fire, I... I want to take her place! Yes, yes, that's it, I want to take Isabelle's place, take James's cock between my own lips... I want to suck him, I'm sick and evil and perverted but I want to taste his penis in my mouth!

The wildly ambivalent thoughts – a battle between the drug-inspired passion, the hypnosis and her basic morality – raced crazily through young Amanda Langley's brain. But the potion and the hypnotic spell were too strong. Passion was winning; that was all that mattered now. Her hand, seemingly of its own volition, slithered down between her legs, her middle finger extended, and she began to draw it up and down the wet, fleece-lined, swollen slit nestled there, tickling the oscillating bud of her clitoris, causing more juices of her lust to flow from the quivering opening and make a damp circle on the couch beneath her trembling buttocks.

She watched Isabelle slave feverishly up and down the burrowing length of the cock of the Lord of Sandaig Manor, the dark-haired woman's body glistening from tiny, rising beads of lust-sweat. Her hand moved more brazenly between her own opened thighs, and the fire in her pussy and in her belly and now in her brain threatened to consume her in one bursting vortex of destruction if she did not have release soon. Her mouth ached, hungered, for the taste of the immense, battering penis, and she envied Isabelle in that kaleidoscopic moment like she had envied no other in all her young life. She had to have James Figgis's cock in her mouth, she had to! It was her turn... her turn... her turn!

"It's my turn, it's my turn!" she heard a strange, high-pitched voice scream suddenly, and then she was scrambling crazily down off the couch, pushing Isabelle out of the way like a wild woman. The dark-haired woman did not resist, but merely released the saliva-slick penis she had so masterfully been sucking and moved aside, allowing young Amanda Langley to take her place between the trembling thighs of the wealthy Lord. Isabelle moved away to a place where she could watch easily but would not be distracting, and her whole body quivered with excitement. Soon now, soon, Amanda Langley would be theirs! An evil, triumphant smile parted her lips, which were wet and glistening stickily with her saliva and the first sticky, seminal secretions of James's tremendous, building orgasm. She settled back to watch.

Amanda Langley crouched where Isabelle had been crouching, between the splayed thighs of the Lord of Sandaig Manor, and she was beyond all reason now. Nothing mattered but this huge, palpitating penis which seemed to sway before her lowered face like a cobra, its head shining wetly from its thin sheen of lubrication, its unseeing eye staring at her like some hypnotic symbol of both horror and pleasure. She opened her mouth, licking her lips, allowing her tongue to stretch out. She had to have it, this great cock, she had to have it swallowed inside her this instant!

She leaned forward and her tongue touched the smooth rubbery head, touched it and tasted the bittersweet pungency of his seminal fluid co-mingled with her girlfriend's saliva. Then she swirled her tongue around the tip's opening, lapping up all of the sticky emission there, and James groaned wildly, his fingers convulsing and clawing at her long blonde tresses at the electric touch of her moist tongue on his pulsating cock. She opened her mouth wide to accept the entire purplish-red head inside, moving her tongue in circular, progressively faster strokes, holding the base between her thumb and forefinger while she tickled his balls maddeningly with her little finger.

Then, momentarily mindless now with drugs, aphrodisiac and hypnotic suggestion, her body hopelessly consumed with the fires of lust, Amanda Langley began to suck rhythmically up and down James Figgis's burgeoning cock, swallowing more and more of his lust-hardened rod into the warm, wet cavern of her mouth, her tongue working with excruciating twirls at the almost-withdrawal from the warmth of her lips. She parted the glans eye with the tip of her probe, widening it so that more semen flowed forth against her tongue. Figgis jerked his hips upward, driving his great cudgel deep and hard against the roof of Amanda's soft mouth. He was moaning in excited cadence now, staring down at her bobbing, twisting head, watching her large, resilient, beautifully formed tits dance and sway from her chest as she rode her mouth up and down his prick, the soft globes bouncing against his widely-splayed legs. He could see her lips clinging to the head of his cock on the upstroke of her head, and he could feel the pressure of his impending come constricting his testicles almost painfully.

Suddenly, as she continued to suck the huge,

driving cock in her mouth, Amanda Langley began to experience a return of rationality. Some of the fog in her terribly drugged brain dissipated, and she realised where she was, what she was doing. And she was sick to her soul, even though she still seemed powerless to stop herself, to cast the hardened flesh from her lips and run screaming for help into the trackless hills. She was alone, she thought dimly, alone and trapped, at the mercy of two people whom she had considered friends but who had inexplicably turned on her, who were subjecting her to the most depraved of demands. Last night had not been a dream, and neither had today; she knew she had been drugged, somehow, knew it and yet still could not fight off the powerful effects. And her cunt still tingled with excitement at the lewd act she was performing.

Oh God, oh God, oh God! her tortured mind screamed. What's happening to me? And why? Oh Alex... Alex... you'll never forgive me if you find out about this! I'm a slut, a whore, to have allowed myself to become what I am at this moment, ooohhh... God, darling!

But these thoughts were jumbled, strange, not at all cohesive. Even as she thought them, even as her brain reeled with torment and sickness, she continued to draw her mouth up and down the rock-hard cock of her host, James Figgis, totally oblivious to her surroundings, to everything but the cock in her mouth and the carousel-like whirling of the images and fears and realisations crowding her brain.

She did not hear the library door open behind her, did not hear the soft thumping of a club foot as it was moved surreptitiously over the floor. She was not aware of the stunted, completely naked figure which slipped inside the room, closing the door silently behind it and then standing there staring with beady, lusting eyes at the carnal scene being enacted before the inglenook fireplace.

The figure was Ganfeld, the deformed and hunchbacked dwarf.

And jutting up from his naked loins in full quivering erection was his immense, thick cock – a cock which would destroy the last vestige of resistance of young Amanda Langley in just a few more moments.

Chapter 6

The dwarf was grinning obscenely, thin rivulets of drool running down along his chin to drop on his bare, shrunken chest. He stood with his spindly legs planted wide, his body tilted to counter-balance his one misshapen foot, his heavy, paunched belly lying over his loins like some ugly, cream-coloured slug. He was breathing hard and stared at the quivering, jerking moons of Amanda Langley's helplessly flailing buttocks as she sucked James Figgis's turgid cock. It gave Ganfeld a tremendous sense of power and satisfaction to see this, to see the proud American beauty grovelling like a common whore before his master – as all women he wanted eventually did – and the still more humiliating experience of being tossed to Ganfeld for his own amusement.

The dwarf began to stroke his huge, throbbing shaft lightly as he watched, drawing the foreskin back and forth slowly. He stared with mounting lust at the contortions, at the winking, pink ring of her anus which he caught sight of now and then nestled in the moist crevice of her white, firmly-rounded young buttocks. He could feel his great, hairy testicles distend and ache and his gnarled hand moved faster along his rigid penis – but not fast enough to cause him to ejaculate, for

he wanted to save his hot, thick sperm for the blonde. Still, he always managed to work himself up to a fever pitch by playing with himself just a little while as he watched one of the women suck his master, Lord Figgis, or one of the other house guests, if that was how things worked out.

Amanda Langley was sucking to please now, totally oblivious to anything except running her tongue wetly around the lubricated head and flicking the tip teasingly into the tiny open slit of the moist glans until she could feel it throb as though it had a heartbeat of its own. Her whole mind was intent on sucking him dry, making his great penis erupt in a gushing fountain of hot male come that would flow into her mouth and throat in a never-ending stream.

Her head bobbed up and down slavishly over the thick shaft of flesh, sucking to draw the milky seed from it until she destroyed Figgis. James, having lost the suaveness and imperturbability of a Scottish nobleman, groaned and twisted beneath her, raining obscenities at the top of her bobbing blonde head and watching with delight the oval-shaped lips straining at his hardened cock-head as though it were a stick of candy fed teasingly to a starving child.

"Goddamn... Goddamn," he chanted, and then seeing his deformed servant at the door, he cried out, "Ganfeld! Just in time! I'm going... going to come soon!

Blinding realisation hit the defiled young woman at that instant. Ganfeld! She heard a soft sound behind her, from the direction of the door, and sensed immediately the presence of the hunchbacked dwarf. Her eyes flew open and she tried to twist around to see if her most horrible fears were true, but James's gripping hands were wrapped tightly in her hair and stopped her from lifting her mouth from his glistening cock. She was imprisoned on his prick, and he levered up with his hips to drive his penis still deeper down her throat.

Behind her, Amanda heard more footfalls and then the high, nasal giggle that sent shivers of repulsion along her flesh. "Well, well, well!" the scratchy voice of Ganfeld chortled. "Look what you've captured, master! A tender little girl, with a beautiful white ass! An ass all ripe for a cock like Ganfeld's to be shoved into it!"

The dwarf snickered again and the blonde wife realised with utter horror the implication of his words. In her mind's eye she pictured the squat, toady face and body of the crippled servant and she wanted to vomit; Lord Figgis's cock in her mouth suddenly became huge and she nearly gagged, and she tried to squirm away. But she was unable to do so, held as she was by the massive hands of the man above her.

Oh God, no! Noooo! her tortured brain screamed. But then she felt hot, excited explosions of breath against her naked backside that made her skin crawl. Ganfeld played at her kneeling form like a sex-crazed fiend, running his hands hungrily over her milky, soft flesh, twisting and squeezing it until small red welts appeared behind the path of his hands wherever they touched. Groaning in anticipation, the wetness of his rubbery lips dropped to her exposed back, slobbering a path along her spine that sent ripples of disgust running to the tips of her labouring breasts quivering under her kneeling body. They descended down toward the crevice of her buttocks which his thumbs were pressing wide apart, his fingers curling down and teasing the wet slit of her vagina between the warm, hair-lined lips that now throbbed involuntarily in time to the cock fucking in and out of her mouth

Isabelle Palermo gasped as the dwarf began the long and licentious quest of Alex Langley's wife's anal passage. She had stripped herself of her own clothing and was sitting in a soft-cushioned chair, her lovely tanned legs parted and letting the black softness of her pubic hair and the forbidden slit of her vaginal tract be bared to all to see... and touch... and abuse. But the two men were busy with Mrs Amanda Langley at the moment, and the eroticism of the scene was too much for the older woman to stand. She had arrived at the stage where her heavy breathing indicated she most sorely needed a release of her own building tensions.

She inserted her own finger into her rubbery, elastic cunt opening, pressing continually inward until her whole hand pressed flat against her pubic mound, and then she began to massage her pink-rimmed channel in circular motions, pressing and expanding her spongy pussy to make ready for a second finger. She groaned and writhed, nearly perpendicular in the chair now as she rolled her erect clitoral bud tightly between the thumb and forefinger of her other hand.

She had recuperative powers that were unbelievable, and this black-haired wife was a nymphomaniac of insatiable desire. James smiled as he looked at Isabelle Palermo's contorted face and watched her mouth open and close in mounting ecstasy. She never ceased to amaze him.

"My dear Isabelle," he said, moaning in between the words and never skipping so much as a fraction of a beat as he fucked the lovely virgin mouth of the young blonde housewife below. "My dear, use... use my...

collection... of dildoes, if you desire!"

Isabelle Palermo's eyes glittered. "Where are they?"

"The cabinet... beside you! Oh, suck my cock, you hot little bitch!" The last words were directed to the increasingly rapid movements of Amanda's mouth, and he was soon lost once more in the heaven of her lips and tongue.

Isabelle removed her finger and with a trembling, wet hand opened the Spanish credenza beside her chair. Yes! There, nestled on the top shelf, was the wooden Phallos Temple from Japan. She removed it and studied the Oriental work of erotic art. Under the slanted roof painted to resemble the female cunt, were seven daikons, painted effigies of the penis. Isabelle shook as if stung with yellow fever at the salacious sight, and then she reached out and selected one, a smooth object of the finest polished wood, its natural grain running the length of its shaft. It was shaped something like a blunted scimitar, one end fashioned to be a handle, the other a perfect replica of a large, erect cock and head.

No one knows how old the artificial phallus is. Clay penii have been found in ancient, prehistoric cities, and the Bible refers to gold and silver images with which the women of Jerusalem committed their whoredoms. The

Roman god, Priapus, was a symbol of life and was a crude representation of the male member, and upon the wooden rigidity of the god Mutunus Tutunus the virginal bride sacrificed her hymen before joining her groom in the bridal bed.

In India, the god Siva is always shown with an erection, and the poems of Herondas of Kos tell of women visiting the shop of Cerdon who had other uses for leather than making sandals. The Greeks carved penii from horn and wood, and in time the word 'olisboi' was given to such items. In Japan, where they are sold openly in stores, it is called a daikon; in France, it's known as a godemiche; in England, dildo; in Italy, diletto.

But whatever name is given to the carved, ornamented, plain or fancy image of the penis, the instrument has given countless women all over the earth and all through the centuries happiness.

It gave Isabelle Palermo happiness.

She whimpered, squirmed, gasped. Faster and faster her hand pumped the daikon with frothing madness deep, deep in her hungry cunt. She screamed and convulsed, her whole belly a sheath to the wooden piston. She stared down at the way her pubic hair moved and her pink vulva grasped at the round sword. The pleasure zones of her female flesh were alive and throbbing, and her hips beat the chair cushion as they worked steadily, insatiably.

Meanwhile, the hunchbacked dwarf held himself back from thrusting his huge penis into the tight ring of the blonde lovely's tight little anus. He purposely tortured himself for the moment when he would bury his throbbing cock far up between her soft, white moons as they swayed gently and defeatedly before him. She was repulsed by him and he wanted her more than anything else in the world. He wanted to feel her squirm and then cry out her need for him, and that would be the ultimate conquest; a proud, beautiful blonde bitch who was horrified by his deformities suddenly turning into an animal and losing all control of herself, forgetting where she was, who she was, wanting, consciously, his overgrown, grotesque cock to fuck her until she couldn't move. The thought raced through his loins like an electric shock.

For a few torturing moments he ground his thick cock around in the narrow, white crevice of her buttocks, pressing the soft, quivering cheeks of flesh around it, enclosing his member like a glove upon a finger. Then he leaned forward and once more planted wet, warm kisses with his twisted lips along the standing ridges of her spine, feeling her tense and shiver and groan slightly around the pumping cock in her mouth.

Then Ganfeld moved his loins up close

behind her and placed his thumbs on either side of the resilient cheeks and pressed out gently. With the natural cunning of a predator, the dwarf knew that she had passed the first stage of physical submission by violence and now the conquest of her mind and spirit must be done by tenderness. Indeed, his unexpected change from pain and brutality to caressing and tenderness caught her off guard in spite of her resistance. Amanda had geared her shocked, nearly benumbed mind to fighting the alien, repulsive invasion; but she was not prepared for pleasure. She was not prepared for the rising desire his touch would bring.

Her buttocks clenched together against the pressure he was exerting with his thumbs, and he eased off slightly, still keeping up a constant easy tension until the straining muscles of her inner thighs slowly tired and relaxed, bit by bit. His triumphantly grinning face was crouched on the same level with the thin, pink folds of her vagina and he watched, eyes gleaming, as the soft, hair-lined lips slowly parted before the imperceptible outward pull of his hands. He saw the slight moisture forming and glistening on the soft insides of her thighs, and with the easing of shock and the fatigue of resistance the cheeks of her buttocks spread wider and wider apart.

The dwarf servant moved his face forward,

careful not to shake the sudden trust building in the defenceless woman kneeling before him. His face was a scant inch from the soft blonde pubic hair covering the tender, resilient flanges of her vagina, and the animal female odour was one of the sweetest perfume that drifted enticingly out of her cavern, better than even it had been the previous night. He swallowed deeply as her secret passage flowered open to his gaze and the soft inner flesh came into tantalising view. It was coral and smooth and wet.

He blew softly into her...

Amanda jerked forward from the unexpected warm, feather-like touch of air on her cunt, and James Figgis thrust upward again, impaling her mouth deeper on his fleshy shaft until she felt as if it would choke her to death. Her concentration on his penis was short-lived as she felt the dwarf push his wet lips teasingly against the wetness of her open vaginal slit. She squirmed slightly and he tightened his hands on her buttocks so that she couldn't move away, and then with one quick rush of his snake-like tongue, he thrust forward between her warm, fleshy vaginal folds.

Amanda gasped, and again jerked forward from the hot, teasing contact in an involuntary spasm of delight. Her buttocks contracted and then opened around Ganfeld's long, smooth tongue, and her breath exploded around Lord Figgis's penis in small, quick gasps. Ganfeld pushed his thick lips closer and began to work the whole of her open loins, sucking and licking at her crazily while she swayed and mewled around the cock fucking into her mouth.

She sucked James's cock hungrily, her mouth salivating as it never had before as Ganfeld behind her worked slavishly, making wet, sucking sounds as he teased her soft, fleece-lined slit. Her pussy flowered and her moistness increased with each further second that the lewd and depraved dwarf sucked and tongued, and lubrication ran in slight warm trickles down the sides of her loins.

James Figgis, lascivious leader of the debauched, groaned and spewed obscenities above her flying head and rammed his cock into her mouth time and time again. Suddenly he couldn't hold his torrential release back another instant, and his penis began jerking motions and spurted a vengeful hot jet of come into her hollowing mouth. She clasped her lips in a tight elastic ring around his shooting instrument and swirled her tongue about the spasming head. She wanted to suck the tormenting man above her dry, to hurt him, to punish him for the bitter humiliation she had found herself in. His groans were of pleasure, however, and with the continual ministrations of the hunchbacked dwarf's lashing kisses on her vaginal area, she was involuntarily incited to still greater efforts. She thought James's release would never end, filling her cheeks to overflowing and making her swallow with thirsty rapidity. Then the hands which clamped the sides of her head fell away and the giant, throbbing cock gave one last squirt of seminal fluid and stopped. The tongue and mouth of the gnarled servant never let up, not for one instant, in spite of the force and reaction of his master's come, for the dwarf knew that his drawing and plunging actions were going to bear bitter fruit in just a few seconds, that his turn was next. "Lick me clean," Lord Figgis commanded.

Amanda Langley, still powered by the potion in the sherry, still determined to follow through and be done with her horrible plight, and becoming more excited by the double defilations of her body – though the latter was subconscious and one which she would later deny – followed his decree. She began at the base where the tiny tufts of pubic hair protruded and began to lick around it with the twirling tip of her tongue, sipping the thin sticky streams that had escaped the tightness of her lips. She could feel it perk slightly under her massaging tongue, and continued her degrading task, praying that she would finish before it sprang to erect life again.

A moment later, it was clear of all escaped come, glistening and wet from her saliva. She watched Lord Figgis's penis, barely inches from her mouth, as it slowly deflated and sank to softness.

"Ahh, that was something," James breathed above her, looking at a trickle of warm, white semen that still ran down her chin. "Absolutely wonderful."

"Now, now me, master!" wheezed the dwarf, suddenly looking up, over the rim of her wavering buttocks. "Now me!"

"Of course, my little man. She's all yours!"

"Nooo!" Amanda cried out, thoughts of her husband suddenly filling her mind. "Please, no more!"

James Figgis looked at her amusedly. He knew that the potion was still having its effects on her physical body, that in spite of her fervent wish of sanctity, her body wouldn't allow her any peace or solace until it was satisfied, until it was satiated from the artificially induced desire for sex. And Amanda, looking up with pleading eyes saw that cruel twinkle and she knew that her pleas would be ignored, that there was no hope for her, even at this point of no redemption. She was sick, she thought to herself, for her whole being still seemed to demand more perversions to be visited upon it, and she still quivered with the tingling sensation of unsatisfied lust. What was the matter with her? Was she really the whore that actually enjoyed the depraved and lewd acts that these evil men mercilessly subjected her to?

"Hold her hands for me, please, master," Ganfeld requested. "She might get a little violent. Her little asshole looks as though it has never tasted the sweetness of a cock before."

Lord Figgis put his massive hands on her shoulders, forcing her head down to the rug, and imprisoned her head between his legs. "You'll learn to enjoy this, my little innocent," he told her. "Ganfeld here is a master at virginal openings."

Amanda couldn't believe what he was saying. She had hoped that the kissing of her vagina, which had been so pleasant and sensual, had been all that was in the minds of the dwarf and his master when first the runt had approached her from behind. Now she could see that her worst fears were to be realised. She had prepared to give whatever was wanted of her, but this wasn't human! It wasn't right! They couldn't mean what they said... they were trying to frighten her, to make her crawl and beg! The decrepit little hunchback wouldn't dare make love to her there!

She clenched her legs and buttocks tightly

together in reaction to the horrible thought. But again Ganfeld slipped down and kissed her in the soft, upturned crevice, licked and sucked the twin hills of her pubic slit, and as if of a mind of its own, as if already trained by what he had so deliciously done before, her thighs automatically widened to his searching lips, and again the juices of her excitement flowed unhampered.

Ganfeld could sense from the building tempo of her body that she was as ready as she would ever be, that all of his previous labours were going to be repaid in full. He wanted her now, to explode inside her rectum with a rhythm that matched her own cries of fulfilment. She'd never just want plain sex again, not after he was finished with her. All the years he had spent in bitter humiliation and subjugation began to bubble over in a boiling cauldron of lust. His long, immense cock ached with the anticipation he was building, while he worked at her loins with his hot, punishing tongue. With some difficulty he slithered to his feet and worked his hips into the now wet and glistening opening of her buttocks.

He held his gleaming penis tightly between his fingers with its blood-filled head poised at the tight elastic opening of her anus, and watched with lewd eyes as the puckered ring flexed like the mouth of a fish gasping for air.

He ached all over from the thought of this lovely young wife kneeling in abject servitude, to be used for as long as he wanted.

"Kneel up," he ordered, eager for the ultimate subjugation of her trembling body.

Amanda hesitated for a moment and felt his hand on her hips jerk them high in the air, making them wave in an open invitation to the cruel ravishment about to begin. Her anus throbbed in abject helplessness.

"She wants it, master," breathed the dwarf. "Oh, look at that hairless little thing pucker and beg!"

His hands grasped harshly at her hips and then the blonde wife felt the dwarf's cock impress itself against the naked split of her behind. It was so huge! She gasped at the first contact, for she hadn't expected such magnitude from such a stunted man. She could never take it all; it would split her rectum in half! She jerked forward, tears of frustration brimming in her eyes.

"Hold her!" gasped Ganfeld.

Lord Figgis's hands dug into her shoulders and he sat heavily on her trapped head. She was wide and helpless before the unnatural onslaught of her loins and she could feel the enormous penis of the hunchbacked dwarf probe harder as with a slight pop the tiny elastic ring of her rectum opened momentarily and then closed back over the smooth rubber head of the dwarf's cock. She screamed and groaned but her sounds were muffled by her position. There was no one in the world who could help her, and all that existed was the excruciating torture of her anus from the shrunken pervert behind her; no escape from the horror and degradation of the depraved attack. The blunt intrusion of Ganfeld's cock vibrated every fibre in her body, pushing the soft, rubbery flesh inside her anal canal in waves of pain and pressure before it. She grunted in submission, relaxing as best she could, until she suddenly felt the coarse hair of his loins smack against her buttocks. The cruel, thick rod was buried to its hilt!

Ganfeld muttered obscenities and gasped with sadistic pleasure and began to fuck without mercy far into the hidden depths of her belly, bringing further sobs of misery from the young wife's anguished lips. She had never felt so soiled or debauched in her life, and her whole being seemed used and filthy. Ganfeld lunged the full length of his deformed body, pulling the tiny pink ridges of her clasping sphincter ring out with the base of his cock as it withdrew for yet another lunge.

Amanda could dimly hear behind her kneeling body his grunts of pleasure, and in spite of the fact that she was hopelessly held like an errant slave before its cruel tyrant, she wanted to strike back at the humiliation and pain that was being heaped upon her. In spite of the agony, she clasped tightly her anal muscles around the huge penis.

"Aaaggg!" Ganfeld groaned. "God, she's tight!" Panting and exerting all the energy of his tiny body, he thrust forward still harder. "So wonderful! Tight... and wonderful, master!"

The degradation was too great. Amanda had to work to end it all, and she began to move backward to meet the forward thrust of the dwarf's penis, undulating her body and swinging her buttocks in tiny circles, clasping and pinching with every cell of her body. She couldn't stand for the indecent sodomising of her rectum to continue one second longer than necessary, and to end it she wanted to make the dwarf come as she had made Lord Figgis do in her mouth a few seconds earlier.

"You can let her up now, master," Ganfeld said. "She's hot to be really fucked!" The dwarf groaned again and surged into her with renewed power. He knew that she was his to do with as he desired, that she was his slave prepared to follow his commands, that there was no resistance left in this innocent young wife whose husband was at this moment a thousand miles away. He would give it to her now as she had never had it – and she would learn to love it – she was loving it now, for as he watched her with beady eyes, her arching back and hollowing buttocks worked as if she was a female demon, her long blonde hair falling over her face and around her neck as she squirmed lewdly and salaciously in front of him.

Lord Figgis, now that his job was finished, smiled evilly at the couple, and then walked over to where Isabelle Palermo was coming for the second time with her dildo. He chuckled and said, "Isn't that a sight to set your blood roaring? Look at me. I've got another hard-on already."

"And...?" Isabelle licked her lips.

"There's another dildo in the cabinet, my love. A double one, with eight-inch phalluses, I believe."

"Marvellous!" whispered Isabelle excitedly. "That means my Lord wants to indulge in sodomy as well, only performed on him. And all the while I will enjoy the other half of the delightful rod buried in my cunt!"

"Precisely, *ma cherie*," he said, and kissed her.

Amanda bucked and churned her body beneath the dwarf, grunting and groaning with him, encouraging the hunchback to end it and fill her behind with his orgasm. Ganfeld sensed her frantic need and rammed her quivering buttocks, gripping her thighs with all his might to pull the tightness of her anal flesh back over his expanding cock. His eyes bulged wide at the spectacle of her young body bucking before him, and the sadistic desire to hurt rippled through him as he jogged with searing thrusts up her forever stretched anus.

Still worse was the realisation in Amanda that the vast hurt, the overwhelming pain his first brutal invasion had initially caused and the subsequent pumpings of his huge organ, had then ripped from her flesh – this torture was rapidly declining, and in its place was a building, warming, seething flame of sexual pleasure. No longer could her conscious mind deny the existence of delight, that she had gotten a great deal of satisfaction out of sucking Lord Figgis to completion, and that the taste of his semen was sweet and lovely and now was a mellow ambrosia in her stomach.

The lovely blonde wife, who had never before been introduced to the wildness of group sex, of having a release of her female desires with more than just her own lawful husband, now had to be honest with herself. Yes, she was being subjected to the worst of perversions and the most humiliating of situations. Yes, the total submission of her modesty before the lewd gazes and actions of these two men and the woman she had considered a friend was too much for her tortured mind to accept. But yes – she was also revelling in it now. Was actually enjoying the tingles of excitement which coursed through her blood and made her bobbing nipples harden and caused her vagina to flow with the sexual juices of desire. She was no better than they, a heathen of the flesh, a slut, a slattern, unfit for the company of decent, respectable people.

"Oh God, come, come!" she chanted in the masochistic writhings of pain and pleasure. She fucked her firm, full buttocks back wildly against the dwarf.

Ganfeld gasped above her and shoved forward, almost tearing through the walls of her quivering belly, and stuttering incoherent words he shuddered his hot, thick come in wave after wave into her rectum. Amanda knelt in front of him, joyfully receiving his sperm until the dwarf groaned and collapsed over her body.

After a while, the blonde wife felt the hunchbacked servant's weight lift from her and his deflated penis slip from the confines of her flooded, expanded anus. She felt wet now, and sore, but nothing like the horror of the beginning. She was no longer a virgin anywhere and there was nothing left for them to do. She had had it all – or so the initiate to carnal love thought. They had debauched her, and she could never forget it nor turn back, and they had destroyed the relationship of faith and trust that had been hers with her husband, Alex. But even though the blight and humiliation would live in her mind from this time on, she knew that she would return. They wanted pleasure? She would give them pleasure – after all, she was destined for hell now anyway!

"I want to fuck you in the cunt now," the dwarf begged, breaking through her thoughts.

"Yes, Ganfeld, darling, go ahead, fuck me any way you like," she heard herself say through her still half-drugged haze and a faint smile played across her lips as she rolled over on the floor. She let her legs spread apart in tantalising slowness, knowing that she might as well learn to fully enjoy her new part, knowing there was no way to go but ahead.

"Master, master!" Ganfeld gasped, unmindful that his Lord was in his own throes of sexual passion, and was not listening. "Master, the hot bitch loves it!"

Amanda Langley, the once innocent, the once naïvely sweet young American wife, let the weight of the hunchback dwarf crawl between her open thighs. She curled them around his tiny hips and even reached down to take his still-hardened penis in her hands and guide it between the swollen, pink edges of her moist and ready cunt. Ganfeld lunged forward and impaled her again on the thick shaft of flesh. Amanda groaned in justified surrender and tightened and drew her legs back and felt his huge, driving penis hit the bottom of her belly.

Yes... yes... she would please them, please them all. She contracted the muscles of her vagina around the surging cock and began a slow, teasing rotation of her hips that seemed to last forever and ever. There was no longer any reality for the young blonde wife, just the pleasure and animal grunts drifting down from the sweating dwarf who crushed her naked body to the study rug, nailing her buttocks to it with his lust-hardened cock like a helpless butterfly impaled with a collector's pin.

Chapter 7

On the second day following that fateful morning and afternoon, shortly past six in the evening, Alex Langley and his boss, Sebastian Palermo, arrived at Sandaig Manor.

Amanda and Isabelle were in the library when they were ushered in by Ganfeld, drinking brandy and relaxing before the ever-present fire in the inglenook. The young blonde wife, wearing a powder-blue pants outfit Alex had given her the previous Christmas, her long blonde tresses piled high on her lovely head, stood with hammering heart by the leather couch as the man she loved appeared in the library doorway. She stared across at him, at his tall, smiling handsomeness – and she felt nothing.

Oh, she was happy to see him, of course. He was her husband, he was Alex, and there was a warmth in her stomach at the sight of him that put a smile on her soft red lips and sent her running across the room and into his arms. But the all-consuming ardour was gone, and in its place there was an emptiness, a void; the total commitment to him and to the life she had known prior to coming to Sandaig Manor no longer existed inside her warm young body. She had changed; she was a different woman entirely.

It was really amazing, she thought with a kind of detached wonder as she hugged and kissed this man who only a few days before had embodied every bit of meaning in her life. She felt absolutely no guilt, no remorse and no shame. It had all been purged out of her, along with her moralistic viewpoints and attitudes, by the thundering, rampaging cocks of James Figgis and Ganfeld, the stunted little dwarf, the loss of virginity of her mouth and her anus, the introduction to pleasures of the carnal flesh that she had never dreamed existed.

These past two days had been a

kaleidoscope of sexual frenzy and fulfilment, a seemingly unending carousel ride of throbbing, ejaculating penii thrust into her pussy and her throat and her rectum, filling her to overflowing with delicious white-hot male seed, sending her spinning to countless orgasms. The hatred and fear she had felt for Isabelle and James and Ganfeld in the beginning had soon become something else, something akin to worship, as they introduced her to newer and stranger eroticisms and delights that put her on a never-ending rocket-ship ride to the far corners of the universe.

She had, in these past few days, become totally emancipated and she knew that and accepted it as an irrefutable fact. She was a new woman, and she was completely at ease in the make-up of that new woman; she had become a hedonist, a lover of pleasure, of the hardened male member, of sex in any form. She had come to believe firmly that there was nothing wrong in the seeking of satisfaction, of physical gratification, merely because it was frowned upon by most of society. Most of society hadn't tried the wondrous deviations from the norm which she had engaged in, and found so enrapturing; they condemned blindly, foolishly, as she had once condemned. They did not know, had no idea – only she knew, she and her new-found friends and confidants here at Sandaig

Manor.

Alex, she thought as she kissed him hard on the mouth, what would you think if you found out what had happened to me, how I've changed? Would you still love me? Would you understand? Would you join me in my new life? Oh, I hope so, because I do love you, in spite of my emancipation, and because I want you with me always. I want you... but the only way I can have you is for you to adapt as I have adapted, because, dear Alex, I can never go back to what I was before. Never. And you must find out, eventually... you must know the truth. I pray that you make the right decision, my darling... the decision that was made for me by Isabelle and James and Ganfeld and – yes, and your boss Sebastian Palermo, for Isabelle told me all about his part in their plans.

But Amanda did not allow her thoughts to show on her face as she stepped back, beaming radiantly up at her husband, and said, "Oh, I'm so glad you're here, darling! How was your return flight?"

"Smooth as silk," he answered, one strong arm encircling her waist.

"And Genoa?"

"A beautiful city," answered Alex. "I enjoyed our stay there. But I'm afraid business meetings kept us from doing much sightseeing," he grinned fondly at her. "Well,

I must say, you're looking very refreshed and happy. Sandaig Manor seems to have agreed with you immensely. Are you enjoying yourself, honey?"

"Oh, very much," she replied demurely.

"Didn't I tell you that you would? What have you been doing with yourself these past three days, anyway?"

"Just relaxing, mostly."

"Been exploring the hills?"

"No, I wanted to wait until you came, darling."

He laughed softly. "We'll go out first thing in the morning. I'm fascinated by the bleakness of them."

Just then, James Figgis entered the library, dressed in one of his many velvet lounging jackets. He clapped Sebastian Palermo, who was embracing Isabelle, soundly on the back, greeted him, then walked over to where Alex and Amanda stood. He extended his hand in welcome.

"Alex," he said, "so good of you to come."

"Hello, James. Nice to see you again."

"I can't tell you how much I've enjoyed your wife these past few days," said the Lord of Sandaig Manor, with no hint of guile. Even so, Amanda felt a faint tinge of red creep into her cheeks, and she looked away quickly. "I'm very glad you both accepted my invitation."

"It was good of you to offer," Alex said.

Sebastian Palermo, his arm encircling the shoulders of his smiling, dark-haired wife, joined them. "How about a drink, James? I'm bloody bushed, driving all that way from London. Hired car was acting up, too. We should have taken yours, Alex, as you suggested."

Figgis said, "Come along to the bar. I'll do the honours tonight. Ganfeld's preparing dinner, and I daren't disturb him while he's creating one of his special feasts."

As they all walked to the bar, Alex whispered to Amanda, "Is Ganfeld that poor little dwarf who let us in?"

"Yes."

"He gives me a creepy feeling. Those beady eyes of his..."

"Oh, honey, he's very nice," whispered the young blonde wife. "He really is. One of the nicest people I've ever met. He's... done a lot for me since I've been here."

"In that case, I'll treat him with extra-special respect," grinned the doting husband.

Drawing Isabelle off to one side as the Langleys stepped up to the bar to watch James Figgis mix drinks, Sebastian Palermo asked in an undertone, "Well, my pet? How did things progress with the lovely Mrs Langley?"

"You mean you couldn't tell by her

expression and her actions just now?" smiled the dark-haired woman wickedly.

"I thought so," Palermo smiled back. "But I just wanted to make sure before I make my approach. How is she taking things?"

"Beautifully, of course," Isabelle told him. "She's totally subjugated, and wildly insatiable. Haven't you noticed how haggard James is looking? She reminds me of myself, when I was won over to the pleasures of the flesh so many years ago."

"You never cease to amaze me, my dear Isabelle."

"Remember, Sebastian, save some of that fine come of yours for your wife tonight. Don't spend it all on the sweet little bitch, Amanda."

"Have I ever denied you yet, my love?"

"No, you haven't," admitted Isabelle. Her smile grew calculating. "I believe I'll have some sport with young Alex tonight. Do you mind, Sebastian?"

"Is it wise to expose him to the truth at this early date?"

"Why not? The sooner the better, I should think."

"Have you brought Genghis to young Amanda yet?"

"No, my pet, we were waiting for you to arrive. I know how much you enjoy Genghis's performances. We were planning things for tonight."

"Hmmm. Well, perhaps we should wait until Genghis and Amanda have become... acquainted before Alex is apprised."

"On the contrary," said Isabelle, "I think it would be the perfect psychological time if he were to witness his lovely young wife and Genghis together."

"Do you really think so?"

"Of course! James will have his cameras set up in the master bedroom, and I shall bring Alex there when things are at their proper moment. We shan't have any trouble."

"How will you handle him?"

"I've instructed Ganfeld to put just enough of his infamous potion in Alex's after-dinner drinks to make him sleepy at first. He'll toddle off to bed, and then he'll become terribly horny; after you've gone with Amanda, I'll bring James in for a quick fuck, as I've promised him, and then I'll fetch Alex when Ganfeld brings Genghis. He'll be so excited from the potion, so shocked from the sight of his wife with Genghis, that he'll put his nice young cock inside me without any trouble at all. After that, he will be one of us, just as Amanda is now."

"Excellent, my pet, excellent."

The Palermos joined the Langleys, then, and the conversation centred on more mundane matters. Alex seemed in very high spirits, laughing jovially, and Amanda felt her heart go out to him. If only you knew, darling, she thought, if only you knew and felt just as I did... what a truly wonderful moment this would be!

The young blonde wife looked over at Sebastian Palermo, who smiled back at her with his eyes shining. Yes, she knew all about Sebastian – he was no different from Isabelle and James and Ganfeld – and she could not help but wonder how large his cock really was, how proficient he was in bed. Her pussy tingled excitedly as she recalled what Isabelle had told her about Sebastian, about how he had made her come ten times in one night with his magnificent penis. Would he ask her, Amanda, to fuck him tonight? She wanted to, after what Isabelle had told her, but what of Alex? She wouldn't forsake her husband, the man she still loved, for Sebastian Palermo – even for one evening; no, she would remain with Alex tonight. His cock was lovely and large, too – how well she knew it! Perhaps Alex was not as accomplished as James or Ganfeld, that ugly, wonderful little dwarf, but it would satisfy her for this evening. There would be other opportunities to fuck Sebastian Palermo... yes, many other opportunities...

They had two drinks each, and then Figgis announced that it was time for everyone to freshen up and change for dinner. Alex and

Amanda climbed the marble staircase arm in arm, and entered the room Amanda had occupied throughout her stay at Sandaig Manor; Alex's bags had been brought there by Ganfeld.

When they were alone, he kissed his lovely blonde wife long and passionately, whispering, "It's been a long time without you, sweetheart. Miss me?"

"Oh yes," Amanda said.

"We'll make up for it tonight, after dinner," he grinned. "I'm really going to love you, honey."

She smiled and nodded, pretending to blush, but she was thinking, yes, you'll love me, but I don't think it will be as good as it has been with James and Ganfeld, my darling, for you see they've had much, much more practice than you have in the art of really making a woman happy.

Dinner was a sumptuous affair; Ganfeld had outdone himself in excellence. There was a steak-and-kidney pie the likes of which Amanda had never tasted before, a superb French red wine and Yorkshire pudding of a gourmet variety. Sated with the delicious food and drink, the four guests and James Figgis retired to the library, where Ganfeld served Grand Marnier in tall tulip glasses, Partagas cigars for the men and strong European coffee.

The fire crackled cosily in the huge

inglenook fireplace, and conversation – sporadic at best with everyone lulled into a contemplative state – died altogether after a while. Alex sat on the couch with his arm around Amanda, sipping approvingly at his Grand Marnier; he did not seem to notice that the silently moving Ganfeld refilled his glass from a special bottle on his tray each time it became less than half-full.

Time passed slowly, and Amanda felt a certain drowsiness that was almost consuming. But her mind was nonetheless filled with thoughts of the flesh, and her pussy ached with its new-found need for the hard, driving presence of a masculine member. She wished Sebastian Palermo would not keep sneaking openly coveting looks at her, for she was afraid Alex would notice – and she kept envisioning the older man's cock, described by Isabelle in great detail, in her mind. Lord, but she wanted to fuck tonight! Perhaps she should take Alex upstairs right now, since she had made up her mind to remain with him tonight – even though, in her new and hedonistic world, it was Sebastian Palermo's cock she wanted even more than her husband's.

Alex drained his sixth glass of Grand Marnier, and Amanda noticed that his eyes seemed to be growing glassy. Sweat had popped out on his forehead. Suddenly, he raised one hand to his face and said in a wavering voice, "Hoo boy, I think I've drunk a little too much! I feel a little dizzy."

"Perhaps you should go and lie down for a while, Alex," the Lord of Sandaig Manor said with elaborate solicitousness.

"Yes... yes, that might be a good idea," Alex agreed. He got to his feet, standing a bit unsteadily. He reached down for Amanda's hand. "Honey, you want to come upstairs with me?"

"Yes, of course, darling," Amanda answered immediately. She stood, frowning a little, and then helped her slightly weaving husband out of the library and up the marble stairs. She did not notice the pleased smiles on the faces of the others behind her, or the quick nod Isabelle Palermo gave Sebastian. She had not been informed of the administration of Ganfeld's potion to Alex Langley in his Grand Marnier.

In their room, Alex immediately collapsed across the bed, flinging one hand up to cover his eyes. Amanda sat down beside him, whispering his name, but he seemed oblivious to her presence now. Had he passed out on so few drinks, Amanda wondered. How was that possible? Alex had always been able to hold his liquor very well. Unless...

She shook her comatose husband several times, but he did not stir. Amanda stood, biting her lip uncertainly. Should she stay here with Alex? He looked as if he was completely unconscious and would stay that way for some time. Should she risk going back downstairs, to where her husband's boss was surely waiting for her? If she did, she knew the consequences. But suppose Alex woke up?

She hesitated a moment longer, then the aching in her cunt became so acute that it was almost a physical pain; she needed release, gratification, her newly-attuned body screamed for it. She decided there wasn't much chance of Alex waking up, not if what she suspected was true. She turned from the bed, opened the door and slipped into the hallway.

Sebastian Palermo was waiting there, smiling a sexually enticing smile.

She walked boldly up to him. "You drugged Alex's drinks, didn't you?" she accused.

"Yes, my sweet," answered Palermo candidly. "And do you know why?"

Amanda's pussy continued to ache horribly, and the petal-like lips of her vagina began to flower wide to allow the moist secretions of her building passion to dampen the crotch band of her brief panties and her inner thighs. "Perhaps I do," she told him coyly.

Palermo licked his lips. His breath seemed to be catching in his throat, and his eyes were feverishly bright as they roamed over her lithe, voluptuous body clad in its clinging, simple sheath. "I understand you haven't seen the master suite as yet, my dear," he said.

"The master suite?"

"Yes. It's very impressive."

"Well, then I'd like to see it, by all means."

Palermo grinned lewdly. "I thought you would."

He took her arm and led her down the hallway, turning at its end to follow another corridor running toward the rear of the manor house. At its end was a huge door, and Sebastian keyed that open, clicking on the overhead light as he did so. They entered.

Indeed, Amanda hadn't seen this particular room before and she was immediately taken with it. It was grandly furnished with old, dark wooden pieces, done in red velvet. There were red drapes covering one wall, a huge red circular bed in the exact centre of the room, and tinted mirrors on the walls. The red motif in the diffused and indirect lighting had a wickedly appropriate atmosphere.

"Quite a room, isn't it?" asked Palermo.

"Oh yes," Amanda said.

Sebastian closed the door behind him and turned to face the beauteous young wife. He began to breathe rapidly, his eyes gleaming, a large bulge becoming prominent at the front of his trousers. "Do you know what we're going to do now, Amanda, my sweet?"

"No," she asked, "what are we going to do, Sebastian?"

"We're going to fuck, right there in the middle of that big, round, red bed," panted the old man. "I'm going to fuck you like you've never been fucked before. Would you like that, my young beauty? Would you like the cock of an old English gentleman filling that tender young cunt of yours?"

Amanda laughed softly. "That might be nice." Her pussy was secreting heavily now, and her brain was becoming consumed – as it did whenever the frenzy of lust took hold of her these past couple of days – with a fiery swirling heat. She wet her lips, running her hands provocatively up and down her sleek sides. "Yes, that might be very, very nice, Sebastian."

His eyes never leaving her face, Palermo began to strip his clothes off. The young blonde wife, meeting his desire-ridden gaze with a hot steadiness of her own, followed suit, stripping slowly and tantalisingly for him. At last she stood proud and completely nude, her golden pubic fleece glistening with tiny droplets of her passion, her large, milky-white breasts rising and falling with the irregularity of her aroused breathing, the nipples rigid and quivering on their peaks.

Sebastian Palermo stripped off his last

remaining garment, a pair of old-fashioned boxer shorts, and Amanda sucked in her breath sharply at the sight of his penis. It stood out from his paunchy loins like some fine old battle standard, thick and blue-veined and faintly quivering. Lord, but it was a beautiful cock! she thought. Everything Isabelle had said about it was true. Oh, she couldn't wait until that passion-hardened instrument was pistoning in and out of her already excitedly trembling pussy.

"Do you like it, Amanda?" Palermo asked huskily. "Do you like my cock?"

"Yes!" breathed the passion-incensed young wife. "Oh yes, Sebastian, it's lovely! A lovely, lovely cock!"

"Lie down on the bed, my beauty," he instructed hoarsely. "Hurry now, I can't wait much longer. Yes, that's it. Now spread those sweet, tender young thighs apart so I can see the mouth of that pretty little blonde-haired cunt of yours. Ahhh!"

Amanda lay back on the round bed, luxuriating in the feel of the red velvet spread, spreading her legs wide as Palermo had ordered. The secreting opening of her soft, tender young vagina was split wide for the lusting gaze of the middle-aged lecher who stood with his turgid cock quivering in full erection before her. She began to undulate her hips slightly, suggestively, and then raised her hands to her rounded breasts and squeezed them lightly, teasing the nipples into further hardness.

"Hurry," she whispered, "hurry, Sebastian, I'm on fire for you!"

With a low moan of desire, Sebastian Palermo knelt on the bed, moving between the young blonde wife's widespread thighs until his face was but inches above her soft, downy blonde pubic mound. His hands pressed down on the smooth flat plane of her stomach and his thumbs slipped into the fleshy outer flanges of her cunt-lips. Amanda sucked in her stomach reflexively as his thumbs massaged for a moment, then pressed outward slowly, parting the soft pubic hair and exposing the full splendour of the moist, red slit of her vagina. The dainty bud of her clitoris was clearly visible, throbbing into hardness just above the stretched elastic opening of her cunt entrance.

Sebastian's head dropped, his long, wet tongue snaking out to flick teasingly at the quivering little nub of raw nerves at the top of the furrow. Amanda's body jerked as the electric contact was made and her legs clamped tightly together around his head, the soft inner thighs imprisoning his ears in a vice-like grip. Her hips began a slow up-and-down movement in rhythm to the probings of his slavering tongue. Soft mewls of animal pleasure came from between her tightly clenched teeth, and in her mind was the delicious thought that Sebastian Palermo was a supreme lover, that Isabelle had been telling her the complete truth in describing his sexual abilities.

Her upper torso writhed like a belly dancer's, back down on the mattress, twisting lustfully to the depraved sucking of her loins. Palermo slid his long, hot tongue deep, deep into the hot depths of her quivering pussy, and Amanda's body arched and bucked wildly under the fevered onslaught. He began to fuck her hard and fast with his expert tongue, fuck her wildly, and her buttocks gyrated with impossible fervour at the delicious, hot probings.

"Ooohhh!" she wailed in lust-crazed delight. "Ahhh!"

Sebastian Palermo lashed furiously into her moist, trembling slit, his hands slipping up over her belly to her full, firm tits, cupping and squeezing them almost brutally while his mouth and firebrand tongue continued the wet assault of her wide-splayed furrow. Then he once more located the quivering button of her clit, and she whined sharply with lust-pain as he took the tiny knob between his sharp false teeth, holding it there, and began to run the tip of his tongue round and round it in continuous circles. Her head flailed in total abandonment from side to side, and the middle-aged businessman opened his mouth yet wider, moving his tongue downward along the smooth, hot, moist slit to the throbbing hair-fringed opening of her vagina once more. And again, he began to orally fuck her, harder and faster, faster and harder, sliding his hot, hard, wet tongue far up into her now hungrily clasping tunnel, listening to her mewling, whimpering sounds of passion as he swirled and flicked his probe around the velvet-like inner walls of her pulsating, soft cunt.

The subjugated, emancipated blonde wife began crooning insensibly with animal pleasure beneath the plunging poker of Sebastian Palermo's tongue. And then, as her buttocks jerked and spasmed beneath the assault, he drew the probe out and slid it licking downward to the secret, tiny puckered ring of her naked anus. She sucked in her breath in a gulping, shuddering swallow, flinging her loins up at him as hard as she could as he brought his tongue into seething wet contact with the forbidden opening, thrusting it into the tight, elastic little hole, splitting it wide to accept his phallic member. Amanda's body quivered uncontrollably, even more so than it had been, beneath the overpowering attack, and her every fibre was paroxysming furiously with torrent after torrent of sensual pleasure.

Suddenly, Palermo ceased his mad licking

of her anus and lifted his secretion-slick face up in a lewd grin. Amanda seemed to freeze, her eyes bulging wide. "Oh God, oh God, don't stop!" she begged. "Oh Sebastian, darling, suck me, suck me, make me come!"

"No, my sweet," crooned Sebastian Palermo. "I want to fuck you now. I want to fuck my large, hard prick far up into that flat little belly of yours. Now, Amanda, right now!"

"Yes, ohhh yesss!"

"Get up onto your knees," commanded Palermo. "I want you to straddle me. Hurry, my beauty, hurry! My cock throbs for your sweet young cunt!"

Quickly, they reversed positions on the bed, so that the paunchy older man lay prone on the circular red bed with his cock standing straight up like a huge staff, the blood-inflated head wet with his seminal emission. Amanda moved astride him, holding his large hips tightly between her soft, firm thighs, her flowered, petal-like cunt poised above his great shaft as she reached down to hold it steady. She held herself motionless for one single instant, and then, almost brutally, she levered herself down hard to impale herself on Palermo's long, hard cock, driving it far up into her screaming, aching belly.

"Aaarrrggghhh!" she screamed with pleasure-pain at the fiery, thunderous

penetration of her vaginal orifice.

Her face contorted with lust, and little beads of sweat broke out on her forehead. Palermo reached up to grasp her waist, raising her up so that just the head of his immense prick was embedded between the soft, hair-fringed lips of her pink, damp cunt. Then he drove her down harshly again, at the same time flexing his buttocks up off the bed in an upward thrust. Amanda emitted another wail, her eyes squeezed tightly shut now and her mouth hanging slack with lust. Using her knees as leverage, she began to slide up and down her husband's boss's hardened cock with slow, measured strokes, feeling the hard, blunt head of his cock pound against her cervix on the downward thrust, feeling it slide out almost completely as she drew upward again, the great rod of flesh filling every inch of her wet, warm cunt channel.

Amanda was only dimly aware, as she rode the monstrous weapon of the middle-aged Englishman, of the door to the master bedroom opening. She could not see, from her position on the bed, the two nude figures who came inside, who moved slowly up near the bed, their eyes glazed with excitement at the lust-provoking sight which they were now witnessing. She could not see the sleek, sweating form of Isabelle Palermo, her hand moving slowly between her own secreting thighs as she watched, nor the strong, masculine body of James Figgis with the throbbing length of his great cock held tightly in his right hand. But she heard their voices as they whispered to one another, heard them and knew who was there – and smiled as she levered again and again up and down the pulsating hardness of her husband's boss's prick.

"Look, James, look!" breathed Isabelle. "She's riding Sebastian's cock like a master! Oh, look at the way her cunt-lips pull out and suck at it as she levers up!"

"She's almost as expert as you, dear Isabelle," enthused the Lord of Sandaig Manor.

"Oh, James, I want you to fuck me! Fuck me while we watch my husband ram that beautiful cock of his up inside Amanda's belly!"

"Yes, Isabelle, yes!"

Isabelle Palermo knelt on all fours at the side of the low, round bed, in a position which gave her a perfect vantage point of the undulating couple on the bed. James Figgis knelt behind her and began to slide his throbbing cock along the soft, hot, wet flanges of her pussy.

"No, no, James!" cried Isabelle. "Put it in my anus! James, I want you to fuck my asshole while we watch my husband and Alex

Langley's wife! Fuck my asshole long and hard, dear!"

The Lord of Sandaig Manor was quick to oblige, poising his palpitating shaft of flesh at the door of the dark-haired woman's most secret channel, teasing the sensitive, secreting head along the tiny, puckered nether ring. Then, without warning, he plunged forward with insane force, sending the full length of his throbbing, hot monster far into the bowels of the insatiable woman, the blunt head tearing at the tight membranes of her anal hole with relentless, merciless force until his loins smacked with resounding fusion against the quivering moons of her upturned ass cheeks.

"Uuuhhh!" screamed Isabelle, and almost immediately she began to buffet back with abandoned frenzy against the familiar cock embedded in her rectum, her hips swirling like a mad woman's, her eyes opened wide and staring at the wildly fucking couple on the bed before her. Her small, round breasts bobbed crazily from her chest as she twisted and undulated her body back against the long, drubbing strokes of the man who fucked into her rectum from behind, his balls slapping with soft, smacking sounds against the wet, hair-fringed lips of her cunt with each powerful forward lunge.

On the bed, the young blonde wife of Alex

Langley rode the hammering cock of the old Englishman as if it were a thoroughbred stallion, and she a long-experienced horsewoman attempting to break its spirit. She hurtled madly up and down the great shaft, her hips gyrating with fantastic, frenetic speed, her hands kneading and manipulating her own breasts while his fingers dug mercilessly into the soft, ivory flesh of her squirming hips. Her long blonde tresses swirled like threads of golden silk around her flailing head, and she made little mewling sounds deep in her throat, totally abandoned now. It wouldn't be long before the orgasm which was spiralling higher and higher inside her erupted forth, and she sought with every ounce of her being to bring about, as well, the coming of the man whose cock she so valiantly rode, to feel his tremendous load of fiery-hot semen spill out and fill her aching, throbbing pussy.

Isabelle Palermo rolled and flung her buttocks back against James Figgis's forward driving shaft, feeling it deep in her bowels, her lips forming a silent scream of passion. Wilder and wilder became her gyrations, until the Lord of Sandaig Manor could no longer stand the pressure threatening to burst his balls wide open. His fingers dug painfully into Isabelle's hips, the nails drawing blood there, and a low wailing sound burst from his lips. His cock suddenly began to jerk

out of control, and Isabelle felt his fire-hot come burst along his urethra tube from the cauldrons of his testicles and fill her anus to overflowing, felt the searing liquid run down along the crevice of her churning buttocks, along the backs of her thighs and then her own thundering orgasm struck and she cried out once in a high-pitched moan of ecstasy as her orgasming pussy added more flowing juices to those of Figgis's pooling on the carpet beneath their heaving bodies.

Amanda heard James's strangled cry of release behind her, and knew that she and Sebastian both could not last much longer. Her body became a dervish of motion as she flashed her clasping, kneading pussy up and down the hammering piston of the older man. She was pinching her nipples painfully now to heighten the tremendous desire in her loins, and her head was thrown back like a contortionist's with the muscles of her slim throat stretched taut. Palermo had his hands hooked with one palm on each inner thigh, on either side of his thundering cock, manipulating the soft, wet flesh as she drove down harder and harder on him.

And suddenly, Amanda was there. She was there! She screamed, "I'm cominnnggg, aaahhh, ohhh!" and then seemed to freeze on the impaling rod of Sebastian Palermo, remaining immobile with his great cudgel buried far up in her belly for a single instant. Then she began to flash up and down his cock with unbelievable motions, chanting incoherently as the full gasping extent of her magnificent orgasm struck her and sent her into mindless spiralling bliss.

The sight of the coming young blonde girl above him was the last and final trigger of Sebastian Palermo's own climax. "Oh Jesus, oh Jesus, I'm coming too!" he suddenly howled, heaving up to meet young Alex Langley's wife's every downstroke as the first hot, needle-like spurts of his sticky-white load jetted into her tightly-gripping cunt, to mingle with the enveloping juices of her orgasm and flow out moistly around his wildly jerking rod. The fluid made pools of glistening wetness on his belly, and on the bed beneath his churning hips, and Amanda almost squeezed blood from her own nipples in the mindless throws of her fantastic climax.

And then it was over for both of the sweating, heaving partners on the bed, and Amanda collapsed forward over the sated form of her husband's boss. She lay like that, with his cock slowly deflating inside her sperm-filled pussy, cradling her head on his hairy, paunchy chest. Oh God, how good, how wonderfully good! she thought. Such a marvellous cock, Sebastian, I love it and I'm going to want it again and again and again...

Yes, I want it again – right now! Right this very instant! Oh dear Lord, I'm as insatiable as Isabelle! I have to have him again... I have to!

"Sebastian," she whimpered, "please get hard again. I'm going mad inside for you. Please get hard and fuck me again, please..."

On the floor, James Figgis watched, alone now, for Isabelle had slipped out of the room almost as soon as his deflating cock had withdrawn from her backside. But now his penis was stirring again, coming to life with the lewd words of Amanda Langley on the bed. Now was the time! he thought. The time for the crowning moment in the full and complete carnal conquest of young Amanda Langley!

Grinning, he looked in the direction of a closed door on the far side of the room – a door which did not open on a closet, as one might expect, but which opened instead on a set of stone stairs leading down a long passageway, which in turn opened on the garden outside; it had been built as an escape passage by one of his ancestors.

He cried out in a deep voice, "All right, Ganfeld! Now!"

The door suddenly swung open, and there stood the grinning, malformed dwarf who had been waiting and listening the entire time to what was happening inside the red, mirrored bedroom. He was naked, his thick cock standing at attention, and his right hand was hooked in the collar chain of the great ape known as Genghis!

The animal was jumping up and down nervously, its huge, hairy body quivering and its tiny, almost intelligent eyes shining with what might have been lust. And jutting outward from the ugly, furry belly of the ape, in frightening black hardness, was the same throbbing monstrous cock which Amanda Langley had seen two days before in the animal's stone hut.

Chapter 8

Alex Langley had tossed and turned, writhing in the grip of some odd, heretofore unexperienced sensation. He had drunk too much, he thought, had become woozy and thick of tongue as he always did when he'd over-imbibed, and as he had in the past, the lethargy of sedation made him want to sleep.

But this time the liquor was keeping him awake, rather than soporifically inducing him to shut his eyes and dream. There was a weird agitation in his belly, a burning fire in his loins, which, when he allowed himself to think about it, seemed to make his penis tingle and his testicles ache. To be without a woman for three days.

He sat bolt upright. A woman! What had made him think in terms of a woman and not his wife! It was Amanda he had been without, only Amanda, his lovely, trusting, innocent wife – and to think in terms of making love to just any female was wrong! What would Amanda think if she knew his thoughts? He blushed in the darkness.

But still his body refused to honour the purity of his intentions. Images of hot, squirming female bodies filtered through his drugged mind, and he groaned and tossed and turned. The bedsheets pressed against his naked skin, tantalisingly soft and smooth as his cock and testicles came into contact. His limp member began an involuntary rise, an unwanted erection, yet one he was powerless to control.

Then he noticed that the bedroom door was slowly opening, that the dim light from the hall was spearing across the floor. He tensed. "Is that you, Amanda?" he whispered. His penis gave a compulsive shudder at the idea of his blonde wife coming to bed, coming to sheathe her husband's throbbing sword with her warm, pulsating cunt.

There was a shadow now, a silhouette against the light. Alex stared at it as the black shadow became larger, bolder. It contained the curves of a woman. A naked, smooth-skinned woman, standing by the door, just out of his vision, his touch.

"Honey?"

Then there was the firm, white flesh of the woman as she stepped into the room. Alex gasped in shock, bewilderment making his face form into frowning lines. "Isabelle!"

The black-haired woman was like a Valkyrie in the spotlight of the hall. She stood spread-legged and proud, her firm, high breasts outlined like the crests of moons; her nipples, hard and jutting, were etched in clarity. The soft, triangular patch of her pubic hair was evident, and the filtering light caught the stray pubic curls which were between her velvet thighs, and Alex could even make out the pink, excitedly swollen ridges of her vaginal lips.

"Isabelle! What... what is this?"

"I want you to fuck me, Alex."

Alex was shaken to the core of his being. The obscene request was like fire, her magnificently displayed body like a torch to his already ignited passions. His body broiled with sudden waves of lust, as if it was triggered to its complete pagan yearnings by the woman's naked entry.

"No..." the young husband groaned, trying to control the surge in his blood. What was the matter with him, for God's sake? He had never wanted another woman, not after having met and married Amanda. Yet here he was, his cock in full and painful erection, tenting the thin sheet for her to see, to know. He forced his brain to reject the adulterous proposal. "No, Isabelle, it's not right!"

"Alex..."

He was helpless under the influence of the potion, and the lewdly smiling Isabelle Palermo knew it. She approached the bed confidently. "I've wanted you to fuck me for a long time," she purred, looming over him, cradling her breasts with both hands. "I've wanted that strong cock of yours – the one I can already see growing with anticipation – and I've wanted to give you my body, all of it to do with as you will. Take me, Alex; take me now!"

Alex Langley groaned and tried to turn away, but some powerful force held him there, fastening his eyes on the writhing, seductive beauty of his boss's wife. Saliva glistened around his lips and his body shook.

Isabelle sat down on the bed and slipped one hand under the sheet. She smiled seductively, and then clutched his jerking cock with a certain finality... moving into a knowing and gentle massage.

Alex sucked in his breath as he felt her skinning his penis back so that the pulsing, red-hot head literally popped out from the thick foreskin. He squirmed around on the bed, drawing his legs up and then flat out, shudders of uncontrolled desire running rampant through his marrow.

"Oh God, oh God, oh God..." he moaned, now completely at the mercy of the older woman.

Isabelle used her other hand to slide the sheet down to where his cock was finally exposed to view. The cooling night air rushed against it, and then his boss's wife bent down and thrust his erect shaft deep into the warm, wet confines of her mouth in one, long, continuous movement. She began to suck, causing him to pant and heave his thighs upward involuntarily as the soft, clasping flesh of her mouth sent a wild spasm wracking through him. She drew slowly up and away until only the head was clasped by her oval, teasing lips.

Alex could hardly breathe. His penis throbbed with hardness and as much as he hated himself for it, as much as he knew that come tomorrow and the facing of his own, trusting wife he would be suicidal with remorse, he knew that he had to have this raven-haired bitch, this wife of his own superior. Isabelle was stroking his cock tenderly now, working the heavy, blood-engorged rod up and down as thin droplets of lubricating fluid seeped from the tiny opening. Alex cursed himself for his lack of control. He had been thinking of having a woman, any woman, and now his perverted wish had been fulfilled beyond his wildest imagination. Knowing he was sick, knowing this was wrong, was not having the icy effect of stopping the rush to copulate in adulterous frenzy, and that made him all the more chagrined. He stared down at the wildly pumping hand of the lust-crazed woman, saw his own cock in frantic response, his mind, drugged and shocked, capitulated entirely. He was going to have to release the pressure in his balls, soon – now! – and he was going to take her, take this woman and fuck her just as she had asked. Either that or he was going to burst!

He tried to grab her in his arms, drag her down to him, but she wouldn't let him. "No," Isabelle said. "Not here."

"Why?" Then Alex thought he knew. "Yes, Amanda! She might enter at any moment."

"My room. Come." She rose, her hand still tightly wrapped around Alex Langley's aching prick, and as if her grip was that of a choke collar around his neck, he blindly followed without hesitation. He stumbled shiveringly out into the long hall, a sigh escaping him as he saw that it was empty. He hurried after her, watching her firm yet full, rounded buttocks undulating provocatively before him. He groaned, all of his moral and logical senses drowned out by the overwhelming carnal desire the potion had infused in him.

She led him directly to the master bedroom, knowing that the timing would be just right. Her husband had just finished spewing his sperm into the young wife of the man whose cock she now held, just as she and Lord Figgis had finished fucking to simultaneous orgasms, and as she had slipped out of the one door to fetch Alex Langley, Figgis was calling for the dwarf to bring in Genghis by the other door. Things should be merrily on their way by now, she gleefully thought, and opened the door.

She stood to one side of the entrance while Alex crowded in behind her, his hungry cock pressed hotly into the crevice of her buttocks. Alex looked over her shoulder, his loins throbbing like rampaging waves of a stormy surf as Isabelle rotated her buttocks and ground back against his penis. Unconsciously he reached around then squeezed one of her breasts, tweaking her nipple between forefinger and thumb until the woman winced in smiling pain.

He tried to peer into the dim room, lit as it was only by ruby lamps. Everything seemed to be a blur at first, and then he made out recognisable forms. There was Lord Figgis, naked! And Ganfeld, with so huge a cock to the relative size of his slight body that it hung down almost below his knees in soft state – which it most certainly was not now! And, horror, there was his boss, Alex saw, Isabelle's husband, Sebastian. They were all standing around a satin-sheeted round bed of massive dimensions, urging on a small, muscular man wearing a fur coat. No... Alex squinted, his eyes accustoming themselves. No, it was an animal! A small ape! And the brute was on top of... was slobbering over... was making the motions of intercourse with...

"Oh, Jesus Christ!" Alex Langley blurted unintelligibly. "It's Amanda! My wife's being fucked by an ape!"

* * *

"Sebastian," Amanda Langley whimpered, "please get hard again; I'm going mad inside for you. Please get hard and fuck me again, please..."

Sebastian Palermo chuckled. He had filled this beauteous young wife's cunt to the brim with his thin, quick spurts of come, he had gleefully watched the blonde girl trying not to lose a drop of the hot, lust-inciting fluid as her vaginal lips clenched his cock in a desperate effort to keep up with his ejaculating penis. And, after his prick had throbbed out the last remaining streams of warm, sticky sperm, Amanda had desperately moved all the way around and took his deflating shaft in her mouth.

And now she was begging for more. He heard the call by Lord Figgis for Ganfeld and Genghis, and knowing what was in store for the once innocent, now gluttonous woman on the bed, he rolled from her and stood up. "In due time you will be fucked, Mrs Langley." He laughed harshly. "Mrs Langley!" he repeated contemptuously. "Mrs Langley, my beauteous American bitch."

"Dear God, haven't I done everything you wanted? Why do you torture me so?"

"Be patient, Amanda," her husband's boss replied, grinning sardonically and once more falling into using her familiar name. "We have something extra special for you. A treat, because you have been so good. Isn't that right, James?"

"An understatement, my good man," was the smiling reply.

God! What now? What more could be done to me? I don't care what they do to me... my cunt is on fire! I'm going out of my mind! The lovely, drugged wife reached down between her legs and massaged her own ravaged clitoris in an effort to relieve the screaming agony swirling around deep down in her belly. I've got to be fucked! My God, why do they hold off? Please... please...!

She only dimly heard the command

to Ganfeld, and what penetrated her ears never reached the conscious part of her mind. Instead she gazed smokily upwards at the mirrors over the bed, seeing the sheer, wanton desire reflected in her eyes from the glass, and she writhed more lasciviously, uncontrollably. She saw herself stroking her own cunt-flesh, manipulating the tiny pink erection of her clitoris. Eventually she let all of her fingers play there in the opening within the flushed lips of her contracting pussy, slowly widening the edges, and she slipped both index and middle finger in and out smoothly between the lubricated folds. Her facial muscles tightened and she entertained two more fingers and heard and saw them disappear with soft, wet, sucking sounds. I don't care! I really don't care now!

She became possessed with her own body. It was beautiful and she knew that she was flushed and straining for a climax. She groaned in frustration as her fingers thrust deeper and harder, but they were not enough. Desperately, she realised that they wouldn't bring her to orgasm this time, that more was needed, yet her hand beat on with insane staccato against the sheets.

And then suddenly the slight, grey head of Lord Figgis bent over her, blotting out her own image in the mirror above.

"Are you ready, my love?" he grinned satanically at her.

"Oh, yes... yes," Amanda moaned. "You're going to fuck me. Good..."

"No, not I," Figgis said gleefully. "Genghis!"

Amanda suddenly came back to reality as she heard the name. She looked at the foot of the bed then, to where the naked dwarf stood snickering, holding the end of a golden chain. And at the other end, fastened by a throat band, was the excited, but grotesque, form of the ape she had seen before! Amanda felt her stomach completely turn over and a deep, piercing wail escaped from her throat. The grinning monster was the most horrifying sight she had ever witnessed, its evil black eyes darting at her as though searching for something to fasten its great, leathery paws on and shred. She jerked the back of her masturbating hand to her mouth.

The massive beast growled, annoyed by her sudden action and shrill scream, and she instinctively stifled another cry for fear of taunting him further. She froze... her thigh still spread not daring to move lest it attack her. The monster beast growled menacingly at her again, his great, simian head just above her defenceless loins.

Amanda tried to slowly wriggle away then, the beady, lustful gaze of the brute frightening her. "Don't let it touch me! Don't let that animal touch me!" she whimpered.

"It's too late," Lord Figgis said contemptuously, and grasped her shoulders as he had when Ganfeld had sodomised her, the strong, sinewy fingers digging harshly into her skin. He loomed above her, his eyes void of pity. "Genghis likes you, my dear."

As if in some sympathetic response, the gargantuan ape shifted slightly on his large, padded feet, and Amanda saw that his animal cock was in full erection again, just as it had been when he had sighted her for the first time in the stone hut. Amanda drew her thighs together in anguished fear, her mouth dropping loosely open as she stared at the gigantic lust-hard penis in astonished disbelief. It was scarlet and looked inflamed as it protruded from its furry covering, a long and rigid shaft with a tapered head and seminal fluid secreted expectantly, and a bulbous base that was double the already incredible girth of the penis. And distended below, pulsing with heat, were the simian testicles, churning with alien sperm-seed meant to be pumped deep into her cringing vagina.

"Please... please don't," she pleaded, but her whimpers fell on deaf ears. She looked up, first at the beast, and then cast pleading glances at Figgis, Sebastian Palermo on her other side, and then at the hunchbacked servant. But all shone features of cold, excited lust, cruel and unyielding, boring into the very depths of her soul.

"Oh God, no, I mean it," the helpless young woman moaned. "I can't do it. I just can't!"

"Relax, and you may find you enjoy it," Palermo crooned into her ear. "My lovely wife, Isabelle, adores the taste of it inside her."

"Up, Genghis!" commanded Figgis, and Ganfeld flicked the chain. The animal flexed its hairy shoulders and beat its chest once, and then advanced on the prostrate girl who was frozen to the bed, immobile by the terror of the sight and of what was to come. Amanda tried to move away, but couldn't, even when she felt the brute's hands creep across the flesh of her thighs and stomach. Genghis grunted excitedly, and she could see his lusting animal eyes between the valley of her breasts and see his wide, flaring nostrils flex with the scent of her female cunt, and his rubbery lips pull back and bare his teeth like a giant, snarling mastiff.

She wanted to scream out again, but the paralysing fear held her motionless, her flesh crawling in abhorrence from the strange touch of the human-appearing beast. Her body struggled to sink deeper into the mattress in escape, but it was useless, for what little

she might have done to avoid contact was stopped by the imprisoning grip of Figgis and Palermo.

There was no sanctuary from the impending rape of her helplessly open cunt.

The weight was heavy upon her, for the brute rested all of his body upon hers, not holding himself up slightly as a man would. Low, whining pleas droned almost incoherently from the distraught housewife between clenched teeth.

"Oh God! Get him off me! Please get him off me! Please! Please!" Her head whipped from side to side, her torso straining against the hands holding her. "Oh God, get him off me!"

There was no thought of resistance left, only the revulsion from this horrible beast hardened to violate her female sanctity. Her body shuddered, for she knew that she was at their mercy. She could fight against pain or even humiliation – but not this – not this horror – that was asking too much. Only death would be better and she would gladly have killed herself that very minute to escape her fate, but there was no way.

"Please! Get him off me!"

Lord Figgis laughed and Amanda's heart sank. There would be no way of avoiding the animal cock straining to worm its way into her tender flesh.

The blonde wife pressed her thighs tightly together, attempting to hold back the squirming penis trapped between her legs. She could feel the slipperiness of Genghis's thick cock sliding against the hollows of her soft inner thighs, and the ape's head pressed forcefully against her breast and she felt the sudden, excruciating pressure of the brute's large lips sucking savagely at her tender nipple. She kicked out automatically with her long, smooth legs, attempting to dislodge the hungrily sucking mouth, and Genghis sank triumphant between her legs as they involuntarily splayed open, his hardened ape-cock safely embedded against the pink, nervously twitching lips of her cunt.

Half sobbing now, Amanda shifted her trembling buttocks in a futile effort to evade the scarlet, up-thrust organ, and the animal prick missed, the blindly searching prong sliding beneath into the soft, hair-crested crevice, rubbing menacingly against her exposed anus. The hot, wet shaft jerked again, and this time slipped up to rub along her vaginal cleft and tease against her inflamed clitoris.

Lord Figgis held his breath, as did the other two spectators who stood rigidly beside the bed, watching the massive ape buck frenziedly at the blonde girl's buttocks, attempting to skewer her onto the still growing tip of his mammoth, glistening prick. Abruptly, the animal bared its fangs and growled loudly in obvious frustration.

His animal desire, his intense anger, chilled Amanda. In desperation and fear that she must submit, she reached between their bodies and grasped the slippery rod of animal flesh and gritting her teeth bravely, guided the point of it into her open cunt, spreading the pink, fearfully pulsating slit wider with her other hand.

Groans of licentious arousal filled the bedroom as the giant beast jerked forward and with a wild, jungle grunt buried his alien cock deep into the lovely wife's pink, grasping young pussy. It slithered into Amanda with a hard, cunt-splitting rush until suddenly it was interred to the bulbous hilt, then the chimp grunted and levered again and his hairy, simian balls and matted hair smacked hard against her smooth, upturned buttocks.

She thought that she was torn asunder, that the surge of the monstrous animal cock had been a battering ram that would worm all the way through her and come up out of her mouth. She howled crazily, lost in the fever of pain and agony. The ape, wild now with his total conquest of the white, naked flesh of the young girl hopelessly impaled beneath him, slaved relentlessly on, gurgling and making deep guttural sounds in its throat, pausing sporadically to lunge in an especially long, spearing jolt. Amanda spasmed convulsively as she writhed in torment under the well-trained beast's drubbings, the whole world spinning around in her shattered mind.

She had begged for more, and they had given it to her, all right. The long, rampaging cock that was now buried unmercifully in her belly was all those cocks of the past three days that had fucked her into madness merged into one. She was suddenly delirious now, and she screwed her cunt up and down with wild, vengeful strokes, attempting to destroy it as it had her. She pinned her legs back, her knees touching the hips of the wildly fucking animal, wanting now to take all of the punishment the beast could inflict. The maddening slap of its balls against her naked anus drove her to wilder insensibility.

"Aaaag! Aaaaag!" she groaned as the chimpanzee ground its animal loins so fiercely into her flesh that it caused her feet to jerk spasmodically into the air, and her toes to curl. The thin walls of her moist vaginal tunnel bloated with the sperm-heavy ridge of Genghis's cock as it slid smoothly in and out like a well-oiled piston. She was completely impaled, and groaned like a lost banshee as the juices of her masochistically dilated pussy ran down between her legs and lubricated wetly her desperately straining asshole and the soft bed below. Abruptly, wild, babbling half-shrieks and grunts streamed from the dumb beast's thick lips, and it salivated excitedly on her dancing breasts, as it worked like the vicious tropical beast that it was, the primeval lust of the jungle motivating it beyond all recall.

* * *

Alex Langley stared at the lewd exhibition in unblinking, fascinated horror. Christ, was that his lovely, modest young wife? Was it possible? He mumbled something incoherently as the black-haired vixen beside him began to stroke his still-hard cock, and in spite of himself he found that he watched the obscene coupling of his young wife and the ape with lurid concentration. She was completely enslaved by the huge beast panting over her, her trembling body spreadeagled on the bed!

Alex gulped aloud, not looking at his beautiful companion as Isabelle took his hand and insinuated it between the moist lips of her own pulsating cunt, but rather continued to stare unbelievingly as Amanda twisted and writhed and reached up with her hands to pull the humping buttocks of the animal tighter between her locked thighs. Isabelle Palermo said something to him which he didn't hear and began to grind her own gaping pussy against his hand and then back against his cock, using her hand to guide the shaft to her wet, hungry hole, simultaneously stroking and massaging his cock more vigorously. But Alex was still too engrossed with the incredible, ramming attack on his defenceless wife a few feet away. God Almighty!

Then Isabelle could stand it no longer. She bent over and ground her thighs and buttocks back against his hips, and in doing so, impaled herself on his hard, blood-inflated penis, letting it surge up into the full length of her seething vagina.

"Fuck me, Alex! Ohhhh! Fuck meeee!"

Alex obediently began to drive into the luscious wife of his boss, losing all sense of purpose beyond what the potion had instigated in him as the lewd, rutting sight of his wife being willingly fucked by a wild jungle animal blasted through his mind. He wanted to scream, to cry, to howl out his torment and rage and incomprehension.

Lord Figgis was squatting beside the bed now, his hands having released the now delirious young blonde, knowing that no further help would have to be given Genghis. "She was a good fuck," he breathed in excitement.

"Yeah," Sebastian Palermo agreed. "Look at her cunt go now, though, just begging for animal cock!"

The evil conversation lashed the tortured

mind of her husband still more. How goddamn innocent had he been, Alex moaned to himself. She's been fucked by others, but God knows how many! Alex viewed the nightmarish orgy in distant incomprehension. Amanda, his wife, getting fucked by a wild ape in front of all these others! He had never dreamed of such depravity – and what he had thought to be his sweet, puritanical wife was at the very core of it! His brain reeled with insanity.

Goddamn her! God damn her to hell! He had to punish her! He had to strike out and soothe the misery of his soul – and the only way he could, the only way he wanted to, was by joining in the lewd pillaging of her body, to take her and extract his vengeance by fucking her too, like the hot little whore she really was!

"Get off me! Get off me, you bitch!" he screamed at Isabelle, and mercilessly wrenched the panting woman from around him and threw her to the floor.

"Alex!" she wailed plaintively, and tried to grab his leg, but the husband was already leaping to the bed, brushing aside Sebastian Palermo with a cuffing blow.

"I'm going to fuck you!" he yelled at his wife. "Do you hear me?"

"Ohhhh!" moaned Amanda, as his words penetrated her mind. "Alex! Oh my God, Alex, it's you!"

"Damn right it's your husband, you fucking whore!" He could contain himself no longer, and he kneeled in front of her face, unmindful of the crazed hairy form pumping with grunting frenzy but scant inches away. Alex held his extended cock in front of his wife's face. "Eat it! Eat my cock! Suck me off while you're getting fucked."

A low, dragging moan came from Amanda's lips as she realised through her fogged mind that her husband had discovered her secret, that she was now barren of the last vestige of her pride. She reached out one hand and guided Alex's cock to her waiting lips, turning her face so that she could get all of his penis – a penis which up until now she had puritanically avoided having near her mouth.

Alex Langley swung his head from side to side and he rammed his cock to its hilt into his wife's wide-stretched mouth.

* * *

Amanda wanted to be ripped apart by the twin cocks in her. She wanted to die with the mortification and humiliation and utter despondency that filled her, but as she sucked her husband's cock greedily, tugging at it with hollowed cheeks and running her tongue with swirling abandon over its pumping head and shaft, great, huge waves of delicious feeling raced through her instead. She was enjoying the carnality of man and beast inside her! Her entire body was like an expanding balloon, growing – growing – ready to burst into a thousand pieces, sandwiched between two poles of hardened male flesh, one kneeling beside her face, the other with its animal penis grinding deep around in her cunt, and both driving themselves to the point of no return, where they would shoot their hot, scalding sperm deep up inside her.

"Harder! Harder, fuck my cock harder, you little bitch!" her husband yelled, and fell into a babbling frenzy of curses which he rained on his wife's bobbing head in a desperate attempt to empty both his aroused physical needs and his tortured mental anguish into her.

Amanda sucked wildly; she was cock-filled again, her body was being invaded and the debauch seemed to drive away the horror of her position. This was all that was real now, there was nothing else as the rising spiral of her impending climax came to her befuddled ears. She screwed her buttocks back against the ape's pistoning prick like a demon-bitch with distemper, and saliva dripped from her oval lips.

"Mmm!" she moaned in muffled passion around her husband's surging cock. "Mmmm!"

Great hot floods of juice began throbbing

from the walls of her vagina and streamed out in gushes over the cock and balls of the animal fucking her and down between the widespread crevice of her buttocks. She splayed her legs high in the air and as wide apart as they could go to give Genghis's still pistoning cock greater access, and she thrust her loins back at the animal with brutal force. Her nostrils flared and one long, last gasp of breath escaped raspingly from her lungs as though she had been hit in the stomach with a fist. She quivered as the peak of orgasm blasted her almost senseless.

Her jealously maddened husband sensed her climax and drove his cock deep down her throat. He could feel the hot surge of his own come begin in his pulsing balls and then race headlong down the length of his penis and spew wildly into the depths of her mouth, filling her so that in spite of her swallowings, there was a lewd overflow of the white, creamy semen which ran down her cheek and matted in her flailing blonde hair.

The jungle brute, Genghis, suddenly began to froth around his thick, rubbery lips, his narrow, marble eyes glazed over and unintelligible gruntings came from his mouth. He jerked forward and his giant penis spat its hot alien sperm deep into the clasping, pink cunt. Alex watched in fascination as his wife's buttocks began contracting heavily and uncontrollably, signalling the orgasmic upheaval deep down in her womb. Thick, white seminal fluid cascaded from the flowered lips of her lust-tightened vagina, squeezing and milking the cock of the grunting ape, forming thin trails of viscid liquid which ran in obscene rivulets down her uncontrollably flexing thighs. And then the rapidly deflating cock of the great beast slipped wetly from her ravaged passage, and Genghis began to back off from between the legs of the young woman, his needs satiated for the moment.

But it was still not enough for the drugged, totally demoralised young woman. She grunted out the last of her orgasm while demoniacally bucking her beautiful body upwards. Alex clenched his eyes tightly shut, some form of sanity returning now that he had creamed wildly in her mouth. He looked down at his lust-crazed blonde wife and tears of humiliation washed down his cheeks.

"Oh... Alex, darling, love me. Fuck me now... I want more, more..." whimpered Amanda Langley. The ache that was her love for this man was ready to burst her heart. But she couldn't stop herself from her crazed desire now, a lusting, carnal lover of the flesh; Lord Figgis, the Palermos, Ganfeld and the ape, Genghis, had all played their parts too well. The defilement of the lovely innocent wife had been too thorough, too depraved for any reconciliation with all the tenderness she and her husband had shared in the past.

Alex closed his eyes and a wracking sob choked his throat, and he tenderly placed a hand on her fevered brow. His spirit was totally crushed by the horrible experience. Sadness hung heavy in the pall of the sexual aftermath.

Genghis was in one corner now, happily eating his diet of fruits and vegetables, his animal mind oblivious to the scene that he in part had caused. Ganfeld was with him, the proud keeper of the trained beast, his lecherous mind uncaring as to what he had himself partially created.

Figgis looked at Alex Langley and Amanda. "Go on, Alex," he urged in a whisper. "Fuck her like she asks. Get down there and join in the fun. Or take Isabelle, like before. She's hell on wheels. We've got a long night of fun and games ahead of us."

"Right," Sebastian Palermo urged him. "Go on; your wife wants you to fuck her."

"Please, Alex... please fuck me."

But the others hadn't taken into account the true effect such a scene as he had witnessed would have on the young husband, or perhaps not enough potion had been fed him. Or perhaps it was that no manner of persuasion would have worked on the man, that he was too strong for their wiles.

Whatever the case, Alex Langley looked up and around at the glittering, lusting eyes of his tormentors, and said quietly, "No."

There was a stunned silence. Alex climbed down off the bed, his head bent with sorrow, and didn't even look back at the bed where his hungrily writhing wife lay.

"Alex... don't leave me, darling!" she pleaded, and his heart broke, but he kept on, half-walking, half-staggering to the door of the bedroom and then down the hall to his own room.

He was too distraught, too confused, too emotionally shattered to feel or do anything right. He got dressed hastily and tried to shut out of his mind the raucous cries of the dwarf as Ganfeld could be heard clambering eagerly between his wife's widespread legs and Amanda's answering moans of "Fuck harder... fuck faster!"

He stood for a moment by the banister, suitcase in hand, and wondered if he should go back in there and become like they were for the sake of his wife. That by doing so he might find a way in time of salvaging her. But he knew instinctively that there was nothing he could do to save her now. She had found her new place. He would have to go home and find his way in this unforgiving world without her. He started down the steps to the front door. He had never felt so lost or useless in his entire life.

Chapter 9

For Alex Langley, who can be found these days in the small, unnamed smoky bars in Greenwich Village, New York, that crazed night still haunts his dreams. His mind fixes on the nightmare he witnessed, of the wild, excitedly grunting beast and his wife locked nakedly together on the bed, and his own crazed reaction... or of the long, grim trek back from the Manor, across the hills to the first town, Inverarie... or of that first, unnamed pub in which he stopped to collect his thoughts and found that it was easier to keep on drinking than to think.

With his love, career and hope ruined, Alex fled to New York, where he felt that he could at least find anonymity. His first few months were spent drinking away his savings and walking the dark streets waiting for some kind of inspiration or feeling to come back into his life. Eventually, seeing his savings reduced to virtually nothing, he began to write his dreams down in a vain attempt to capture them and remove them from his thoughts. They were quickly picked up by a small but well-known publisher of erotic fiction, which was excited by his incredibly realistic and absorbing stories of wanton women, remote

Scottish manors and bestiality.

He was on his third novel now, yet he could not get away from the theme that repeatedly came up in his mind, and he was forced to relive again and again the obscene perversions that had ripped his life apart. As on that fateful night, in his writings he was always the observer, the onlooker – the voyeur – no one knew the deep truth behind his stories. In the penultimate chapter of his novels he was drawn to writing of a beautiful woman on a huge bed centred in a roomful of people. Guests would watch while Genghis mated with the woman, fucking her from behind like she was a base animal. Completely naked, save for her strings of diamonds, she would cower in submission before Genghis, who, screaming in his pleasure, would penetrate her with his enormous penis, brutally and sadistically it seemed to those guests who came up as close as possible to see the animal's huge, black penis shafting in and out of the beautiful woman's dripping cunt. Her large breasts swung from side to side, and men and woman would grasp at them when they could reach, until the beast and Amanda orgasmed together in a frenzied, sweating mixture of man and beast.

This was all Alex had left of Amanda. He punished her by making her suffer by the beast, making her scream with pain, tears running down her cheeks. But, always, the manuscript would be returned for a rewrite – the woman had to be a heroine; ultimately she had to have loved her subjugation – and Alex would have to write out her suffering and write in her triumph and her pleasure. He could not make money out of the ending he ultimately wanted to write. And so he continued, adding twists and turns to the same old story – just a fantasy to those who avidly bought the books, but a desperate reality for him.

Patrons of the bars along the boulevard which Alex frequents are typical New Yorkers. They've heard it all and seen everything and take with cynicism and boredom the tales that outsiders bring to the brass railing. But they shy away from Alex Langley, sensing in some inexplicable way that there is a deep, black grief which is eating with a brooding, sharp agony at the man, that his uninterrupted silence hides a secret which they wouldn't want to hear even if the chance were to be given. There is a malignancy about Alex Langley, they say, one which festers, and that no amount of alcohol dissipates. They always leave a stool empty on either side of the man, these jaded pragmatists, and they hope that one of these days the man who sits alone and never speaks will move on.

Alex raises the shot glass of cheap bourbon

to his trembling lips and drinks it, mentally toasting for the hundred thousandth time his ex-boss, the ancestral head of Sandaig Manor, the dwarf servant, the nymphomaniac black-haired wife and the ape. Especially Genghis; here's to Genghis. He puts his hand forward again and nods to the beefy bartender to fill the glass again.

Only once in the six months he's been a part of the seamy area has anybody ever seen the tired, rejected man break down and show some of the emotion he has bottled up inside him. Only once, on a rainy night at three am, when there were only two other regular customers and the sleepy bartender in the dingy bar to see it. Alex Langley sat alone as always, way back in a corner at one of the small, bench-like tables. He had just arrived, and the previous occupier of the table had left a copy of *The New York Times* lying open on the table. Suddenly Langley seemed to stiffen, or so the story goes, stiffen as though he had been shot. And just as suddenly one hand crumpled the top few sheets of the paper, and the rest of him collapsed. He let his head rest on the table and he cried. Long, uncontrolled sobs from deep within; the tears of agony unrequited. That was the only sound in the quiet bar, and it seemed to go on forever.

No-one stopped him, no one tried to interfere with the drunk's private hell. At last he lurched to his feet and stumbled out into the miserable night as though trying to escape from a horrible nightmare. But none of them there or any of the others that were told afterwards ever found out what motivated the scene. All they can tell you is that the wrinkled newspaper pages were carefully smoothed out, and the bartender and the customers looked over the top pages to see if the answer could be found.

The pages were the beginning of the social news. There was a half-page spread about a debutante's impending marriage, and an account on the balance of the two open sheets of a very large, very posh benefit party given by one James Figgis at his ancestral mansion in the Scottish Highlands. The benefit was for a foundation interested in studying the close ties between man and other mammals, something to do with heredity and evolution, though the men who read the account in that bar were none too clear on the details.

And there was a picture, of course, showing some of the guests. The picture had taken the brunt of Alex Langley's vicious fist, but it was still clear enough to see that in the foreground was a very lovely blonde woman regally clothed and being escorted by the host, Lord Figgis. Her arm was linked with the Lord's and her other hand held a gold-chain leash. The leash was attached to a young, virile-looking ape, the paper reported; a pet which the young woman, Lady Amanda Figgis, had raised since birth and was seen with very often in the social swirl of upper-crust London.

The men all admired the woman, for she was quite a dish, as they said, and old Figgis was damned lucky to latch onto such a find. They never connected the lady with their fellow drinking bum, never suspected he had ever been to England.

For Alex Langley never gave his name. Not to anybody. He was and still is too wretched of soul even to allow that gesture.

Just a few of our many titles for sale...

Lazonby's Heiress
Little does Alison realise her duties as secretary of Lazonby Hall include being a sexual 'play-doll' for the lascivious desires of all in the house. Mrs. Simpson is Mistress of the Hall in name, but now it's Alison's luscious young body that holds the title!

Helen's Southern Comfort
In the heat of the night Danny watches as his innocent wife is treated to pleasures she has never experienced before by his well-endowed neighbour. So begins a journey of sexual discovery for the Nielson's that takes them to the very edges of extreme sexual practices.

EVELINE
Gorgeous nymphet Eveline embarks on a dizzying path of sexual encounters as she tries to satiate her urgent needs on as many men as possible. Vania Zouravliov's rich and vibrant drawings bring explicit life to this unparalleled story of teenage debauchery

GAMIANI
One of the most important novels to have come off the 19th-century presses, this novel explores one night's abandon by the Countess Gamiani, her lesbian lover and a voyeur turned protagonist. Shockingly explicit, even by today's standards.

Eros and Thanatos
A high-art treatment of hardcore subject matter, this book contains the stunning work of late artist Klaus Böttger. Sex is lovingly, graphically depicted as bodies writhe at the very pinnacle of ecstasy. Contains two short novellas.

The Lost Drawings of Tom Poulton
British erotic institution Tom Poulton completes our trilogy of his work with this set of drawings that were previously thought to be lost. Also contains one of the dirtiest short stories, illustrated by the artist, the EPS has ever published.

The Secret Art of Tom Poulton
The first in the series of Tom Poulton books, this is a must for any erotic library. Containing some very graphic illustrations from this master of his craft it shows Poulton at his orgiastic best. Also contains two period novellas.